ONE
Rule

ELENA M. REYES

SUMMARY

Danger is never hidden in the shadows. It haunts in the daylight.

I've watched her grow up since we were teenagers. This gorgeous little doll—my obsession—even if a man like me has never had any business desiring something so pure. Not that it stops me; I'm her brother's best friend with a past marked by death and a future that promises to bathe the streets of Miami with the blood of her enemies.

In her name. As a future wedding gift.

Because someone was stupid enough to hurt those she loves. And while she gets closer to the answers she seeks, to finding her father's killer, I indulge her while stalking her every move. Let her dig and tempt danger while my finger's always on the trigger:

My angel hunts within the darkness I control while I execute. She has a hold on me no amount of time can break.

Yet someone ignored my one rule:
Most things in life can be forgiven—all except *this*.
Never touch what belongs to me.
And Liliana Armas is just that. *Mine.*

ONE RULE
Was written by Elena M. Reyes
Copyright 2023 ©Elena M. Reyes

Editor: Marti Lynch
Cover Design: Raven Designs

Publication Date: August 28th, 2023
Genre: FICTION/Romantic Suspense/
Erotica Suspense/New Adult
Copyright © 2023 Elena M. Reyes
All rights reserved.

ONE
Rule

playlist

YOU PUT A SPELL ON ME BY AUSTIN GIORGIO
CAN'T HELP FALLING IN LOVE BY
TOMMEE PROFITT, BROOKE
DO IT FOR ME BY ROSENFELD
LUST OF POWER BY GABRIEL SABAN
I WANT TO BY ROSENFELD
FETISH BY SELENA GOMEZ & GUCCI MANE
COME & GET IT BY SELENA GOMEZ
GIRL LIKE ME BY BLACK EYED PEAS & SHAKIRA
DANGEROUS WOMAN BY ARIANA GRANDE
SOMETHING BY THE BEATLES

ONE
Rule

playlist

SINNERS & SAINTS BY ANDREA WASSE
YOUR BODY IS A WONDERLAND BY JOHN MAYER
MIENTRAS ME CURO DEL CORA BY KAROL G
BIDI BIDI BOM BOM BY SELENA
BUM BUM TAM TAM BY MC FIOTI
I'M YOURS BY JASON MRAZ
KILL OF THE NIGHT BY GIN WIGMORE
PUNTO 40 BY RAUW ALEJANDRO & BABY RASTA
OCEAN BY KAROL G

ACKNOWLEDGMENTS

This one is for my readers.
The love and patience you've shown me as I recover from a heat
stroke and then being sick; I've cried a few times.
Thank you for all the messages, your concern, and for always giving
my characters so much love.

You Guys Complete Me.

Also, a huge THANK YOU to my team:

Ana Rita, Marti Lynch, Jennifer Mercer:
THANK YOU FOR STICKING BY ME THROUGH THIS CRAZY
RIDE. I couldn't have finished this book without your help, jumping
in whenever I needed you, and the tough love when warranted.

And lastly, to my husband:
You will always be my favorite nurse. Love you, Boo.

XOXO
Elena

TRIGGER WARNINGS:

This book contains dark elements that some readers might find triggering. This man is brutal and unapologetic, please read at your own discretion.

Contains:
Explicit Violence
Death & Torture
Family Death (Parent)
Some Primal Play
Obsessive Anti-Hero
Anal
Virginity
Some Stalking
Cock Warming
Boss/Employee Dynamic

CONTENTS

Prologue
MICAH

"My precious little rebel," I groan from the foot of her bed, fist tight as I stroke my cock. Roughly. Hungrily. Taking in the rhythmic rise and fall of her chest under the soft glow of a nearby salt lamp. How she grips a shirt I recognize as mine, an old championship baseball memento from high school, in her tiny fist while her mouth gives a slight, seductive pout.

A tiny one; unconsciously coquettish and the cause of my moment of weakness. My torment.

I want to paint that sinful mouth with my come. Glide my seed across the plump flesh as if it were that watermelon-flavored lip gloss she loves so much and I've made sure she's never without.

Because without her knowledge, her every need is taken care of by me. No one but me.

"Motherfuck, baby. What you do to me." Another grunt. Fire licks up my spine; the sharp tendrils run from the soles of my feet to the back of my skull before settling on my aching balls. They're swollen and heavy, full of the need I've pushed back for her sake—this delicate yet sinful doll that I've vowed to protect and make mine one day.

Since the day I first laid eyes on her, Liliana's become an obsession.

A pulsing in my veins.

This ticking that thrums inside my chest.

And even then, as teenagers, I knew there was something different between us.

Because nothing matters more than how she feels, then and now. Fuck the world; her unhappiness has never sat right with me, but I've made concessions along the way...

To her father, who knew and I never hid my intentions from.

To her brother, who gave me his blessing while accepting my promise.

I've let her live and enjoy herself within certain means while I'm never but a few steps behind her:

No male friends. No boyfriends. No dates.

She's never been far from my line of sight.

I've let her grow outside of my overwhelming, possessive grip. Nurtured by my hand, even if she's unaware of my obsession; I indulge her every whim while protecting her from the shadows.

Promises that no longer apply. Not after what happened a month ago.

Another rough inhale, and every muscle in my body painfully contracts; her cupcake scent—this decadent sweetness that comes from her and the lotion she uses—wraps around me like a caress. I'm throbbing while drops of pre-come fall to her bed and stain the tufted footboard inches from where her tiny toes curl under thin covers.

Every pump of my wrist is near punishing, a complete contrast to the battle—how I fight to regain control over this near demonic need riding me closer to the edge. Her every breath is a flirtatious call to come closer. Her little sighs command my next strokes to be harder than the last, tightening to the edge of pain because everything she does is a morbid combination of heaven and hell—a gift and punishment that will one day break the last threads of my sanity.

Slowly. Or maybe it'll be an explosion.

"Doesn't matter either way," I hiss from between clenched teeth, welcoming my destruction as long as in the end, she's my reward.

Mine. Only and always mine.

And I'll start by marking my territory like the rabid beast she's turned me into.

Like an offering or unconscious agreement, Liliana shifts a little more then, and a single foot slips from beneath her blanket. The sight pulls a harsh shiver from me, a head-to-toe spasm while my cock dribbles a little closer to where her bare toes rest. Tiny, dainty, and painted in her favorite shade of dark purple, they wiggle before she resettles, and I bite back a groan.

So fucking adorable.

My body leans over, closer—careful not to wake her as I place a single knee atop the mattress. It dips and redistributes its firmness while gifting me just enough access to her flesh that the next pearl-like drop glides down the sole before disappearing into the sheets below.

Motherfuck, the sight causes a rush of feral pride to settle in my chest.

I fuck my fist to the classical music playing from the surround sound. This is a part of her nightly ritual, just like the melatonin she takes at my doctor's suggestion to help her rest.

They keep her in a deep state of sleep. Enough that I can come and go as I please without her knowledge; she's at my mercy and under my protection.

Soon she'll know. She'll kneel for me and part those pretty lips: tongue on display and waiting for my come.

The music is low; a playlist she relaxes to each night and as the crescendo rises, so do the pumps of my hips. The instruments are being pushed to their limits while my strokes match the almost violent notes. They fill the room, overshadowing my grunts while snapshots of the many ways I want to break her scroll through my mind like a movie reel.

From her ass to her plump mouth, I want to fill each hole until it overflows. Watch it spill out so I can push—

"Son of a bitch," I grit out then as my world stops for a second. Every part of me is held captive as Liliana turns, taking the sheets with her and exposing the left side of her body from hip to those exposed toes. Soft, flawless, tanned skin. Sinuous curves. The crease of her bare ass cheek has me throbbing from head to toe while my teeth gnash—ache from the urge to sink them in deep, leaving a permanent indent on each curvy globe.

My eyes shift, and I take in her pretty pink flesh next. Just a tease of her sweet slit and bare lips.

Liliana isn't spread out for me, but the position is a gift I reward with a brutal tug of my cock. One is all I need for the first rope of my release to pulse from my engorged tip, and I follow it through heavy-lidded eyes as it lands across her foot. *Fuck, that's beautiful.*

But then again, every part of her is simply exquisite.

The next one kisses just the tips of her toes before soaking into her fitted sheet.

And I'm not the least bit ashamed. No remorse.

I don't stop until every last drop has marked my territory before using my semi-hard length to massage my essence into her flesh. From the tip of her pinky to her calf, I gently rub my dick across her skin until I'm satisfied with the slight glow left behind.

"The next time I come, I'll be buried deep inside of you." My vow. A promise that comes out low, rumbling from deep inside my chest as a new track begins to play over her speakers. This one is softer. It feels like the calm after the storm, but this turbulent, posses-sive grip doesn't abate. If anything, it cements the end of my patience. "I'm done waiting, my beautiful little rebel."

My muscles contract as I stroke downward, squeezing the tip and drawing out the last few drops of my release while my phone vibrates inside my pocket. It starts as the final pearl-like dribble clings to the tip—before another shake causes it to meet with her sheets—and then the call stops. Three times it does this; I ignore it each time and instead lift the corner of the fabric closest to me and wipe the last remnants of my come on it.

The perfect mess.

Tucking my cock inside my dress pants, I stretch my neck and cast a quick glance at her bedside clock. It's a little past two in the morning and I'm in no rush to leave, ready to defile her one more time, but stop when the vibration changes to the subtle three quick raps that indicate an incoming text.

With my zipper half down, I pull out my cell and open the last message. The number belongs to someone who knows better than to disturb me; I don't hide who she is to me, but his words are worth the moment of annoyance.

> At the Royce shipyard where Esmeralda is dry-docked. I received the package. ~Isaac

Immediately after reading his text, my eyes shift to the still-sleeping beauty. I take in the slow rise and fall of each breath and her messy, black hair while her plump lips pucker. Then there's the way she still clings to my shirt while unconscious—how soft and delicate she looks while the innocent warmth she exudes calls to me.

It always has, even though I know Liliana Armas is no wallflower.

She's cunning and smart.

Attracts attention and it's not always the good kind, yet it doesn't matter.

I indulge her while stalking her every move. Let her dig and tempt danger while my finger's always on the trigger.

> I'll be there in twenty. Handle the parcel with care.
> ~Royce

I don't wait for his reply. Instead, I bend down low enough to place a chaste kiss on her ankle. There's a little of my come there, but it doesn't bother me. If anything, it feeds my animalistic pride to know it's my scent on her soft skin. That she'll carry a bit of me with her until she takes a shower after her morning yoga session.

One last inhale—I memorize every exposed inch of flesh—and then turn to leave, exiting the room while fixing my clothes. I only deviate long enough to rinse my hands inside the half-bath near the living room and slip one of her hair ties around my wrist before leaving the same way I came.

My phone vibrates again as the soft thud of her heavy wooden door follows. It echoes a tiny bit, nothing that'd wake her, while I nod at the guard standing in front of the elevator.

He's waiting for me with the door open, and I step inside without a word. It's unnecessary. Her security knows the consequences—what I'm capable of—when it comes to her safety.

And as he steps back and the metal door closes, I shift a final glance at her entrance. It reminds me of why I initially came to see her.

Of the attention Liliana's dinner with Luna De Leon and her husband drew.

Of the two cadavers I'll be disposing of before the sun rises.

But she's worthy of it:

Of my obsession. Of my loyalty.

Sweet dreams, my little rebel. I'll see you soon.

Chapter 1
MICAH

A MONTH AGO...

"I'm not a patient man, Alfred," I say, voice reverberating throughout the lower deck of my newest ship. It creates a deep and angry echo in the vast space, bouncing against a stack of empty crates in the corner and then the hollow jail cell sitting unused at the moment. *For now.*

We're out at sea, cruising through the Caribbean at twenty-three knots on our way to the next scheduled port. It's a little past eleven p.m. and many of our guests are upstairs partying or catching a late show—unable to think past their next specialty drink with a little umbrella—while I sit back and watch the man across from me tremble.

Sweat drips down the side of his pallid face while a nervous twitch creates a near-constant jerk of his legs. Then there's the fear in his eyes. They shift around the room, taking in every face while hoping someone will save him.

They won't, though. No one will.

"Mr. Royce, this is just a huge misunderstanding." Alfred lifts both hands up in a protective gesture, as if afraid I'd strike him, and I will, *but* not yet. Instead, I turn my attention to the three fingers' worth of Macallan in my chilled glass. Condensation drips from the side and stains the wood grain of the small table separating him and me, creating a ring that almost makes me smile.

My little rebel hates when people don't use coasters.

She's also never far from my thoughts. A constant reminder of why I do what I must.

To keep her safe. To bring a smile to her face. To be worthy of her.

So she lives in a world where the darkness I control like a puppet on a string never touches her.

"You have five minutes to explain yourself." Voice calm, I tap the rim of the tumbler and from the corner of my eye, I see one of my most trusted men exit the room while another guard starts a timer on his phone. "Time's ticking."

"Please, Mr. Royce...we'd never—"

"Who is this *we* you speak of?"

Catching his mistake, the man shifts again and gives an anxious chuckle. "My apologies. That's not what I meant."

"Enlighten me, then. How exactly did you end up on this ship *and* inside my vault two days ago?" Arching a brow, I bring the whisky to my lips and take a deep sip. The notes of fruit and spices bloom on my tongue, caressing each tastebud while he tracks my every move. While I savor and hum—the touch of wood and smoke weaving in and out as I pick apart different notes—he shivers.

Swallows hard.

Rubs the back of his neck.

Alfred does everything but reply. Not a single word, and with

8

each tick of the clock, my patience wanes to the point where my fingers twitch—I want to put a bullet between his eyes without getting what I need first.

Because he won't be leaving this ship alive.

The sea will take care of him. It's never failed me.

Can't you be nicer, Captain Grumps? Do you need a time-out like in those chocolate bar commercials?

Her voice—her teasing words from just last week after I snapped at a man who tried to buy her a cup of coffee—play in my head. It might've been her way of defusing my anger, thinking my protectiveness comes from a place of friendship, but it was indeed adorable.

The truth is, I'm a jealous asshole with little restraint when it comes to the woman who will one day wear my ring. Liliana Armas doesn't know how far I'd go and have gone to claim her.

But more importantly, at the moment those words fit. She's right.

Instead of striking out of anger, I smack a hand on the table, and the guard keeping track of his five minutes clears his throat. "He has three minutes left, sir."

Alfred swallows hard at that. "You misunderstood me, Mr. Royce. My apologies if I confused you."

That statement gets no reaction from me. I'm neither surprised nor upset by the blatant insult to my intelligence. Instead, I'm finding myself amused and retaking my earlier stance. Leaning back in my chair, I lift my glass in a silent toast because if you give an idiot enough rope he will hang himself.

And he will. The way he exhales and his shoulders relax tell me as much.

Fucking idiot.

Most people have a certain level of self-preservation they cling to in moments of distress. That fight-or-flight response helps most people stay alive, while others negate the possibility of ever being a victim of a crime while knowing their executioner.

Yet most crimes committed are done by someone close or an acquaintance. They know you.

Your schedule. Your weaknesses. Or in this case, someone with a loose tongue coming forward to sell you out for a few dollars. The degrees of separation between you and the weapon that steals your last breath don't matter when the cause and effect come from the same well.

Too bad your partner wasn't smart enough to protect himself.

Because killers don't hide; I thrive in it.

My darkness isn't afraid of the light.

Instead, I dominate both while to the outside world, I'm nothing more than the product of nepotism. A rich man by birth who inherited his father's cruise ship company while never dirtying his hands; I enjoy their idiocy.

I'm not a saint, and there isn't enough bleach in this world to cleanse the blood from my hands. Moreover, I'm proud of every speck. Power comes with sacrifices and knowledge; my price to inherit the position as head of the business was steep, but not something I didn't welcome.

Others' naivete over my persona is what makes me a dangerous man.

I have friends in every facet of corruption, politicians and organized crime alike.

"Who is he?" Three words, and they destroy his illusion of safety.

"W-Who? I-I swear I'm here by myself, sir." His voice is high pitched. Stuttering. "You can check your surveillance systems. There's a camera right outside of—"

"How long did you study the layout of this ship? Who gave you the access?"

"No one. I swear...*fuck*!" The idiot cries out in pain seconds after the impact. At once, the tumbler with the remaining contents shatters, fragments scattering while the largest shard remains in my grip. It's against his flesh, digging in deep and flaying open the top layer of skin while I saw it back and forth, working deeper with each pass.

It's his blood that drips from my fingertips and onto the white polo shirt he's wearing today.

His plan had been a simple one: blend in with my staff and dress the part.

His mistake had been thinking I'm unaware of every single move on and off my ships.

"Liars never make it to heaven. Try again."

"Please." A plea. A pathetic whimper I glare at. "Let's talk this out. No need for violence."

"Now where would the fun be in that?" The bottom edge of the glass sits just about mid-cheek and I move it toward his nose and back toward the ear, creating a bigger, jagged mess. Slowly. No rush as the flesh tears and rivulets of red drip down my hand and his body. "How much time does he have left?"

At my open question, the guard managing the clock looks at me. "Time's up."

"You lost your chance. Bring him in." No sooner has the last word slipped past my lips than my right hand comes in, dragging the accomplice by the hair. He keeps it long and in a bun, but now it's in Isaac's grip while he walks him in. Herbert doesn't look up at Alfred's gasp, nor does he react when the latter mutters a low *Dios mio ayudame.*

Little do they know that I'm bilingual, and God will not help him either.

In fact, the man doesn't react at all, and a second later Alfred understands why. It dawns on him how steep his repayment will be. His business partner's mouth is destroyed. Lips torn and cut, the direct damage from a baseball bat striking repeatedly. No teeth in the front, the small serrated pieces left are sharp and add to the already painful damage each time his lower face so much as twitches.

Then there are his eyes; swollen and black to the point he can't see.

At this moment, all Herbert has to rely on is his hearing, and even the tiniest noise makes him jump.

Herbert's attempt to double-cross me is his downfall. Greed got the best of him.

Dropping the glass, I push the chair I'd been sitting on back and move closer to our new guest, stopping once he's kneeling at my feet. Herbert senses my presence and tries to shift away, but I grip his chin and turn his face toward his associate. "Do you know why he's here, Alfred? Do you recognize him now?"

"No. I don't know this man." Low. Almost indiscernible.

"So be it." It's another lie, and I show him the consequence when I give Isaac a single nod after releasing my grip and stepping aside. A sharp kick to the ribs and Herbert bends completely over now, folding into himself as the force takes the wind out of him and pain radiates throughout his lean frame. The man is no more than five foot five and a hundred and thirty pounds soaking wet—he's not much of a physical threat.

Not because he can't fight or his size hinders him, which doesn't matter when trained, but because this man considers himself the brains of the operation. He plots, and his past partners execute—get their hands dirty.

No fighting technique of any kind. No knowledge of weaponry.

And while Alfred was trapped inside my vault, I caught Herbert trying to steal one of my smaller Jet Skis hidden a few decks up and with access to the ocean via a private hydraulic lift that lowers to just the right depth to unload. With him, he'd taken two thumb drives and a ring box worth more than the life of every person within this vessel.

The ring was commissioned the day I turned twenty for my future bride. Have it with me everywhere I go.

"Name is Herbert Mullaney, age thirty, and a resident of Pembroke Pines. Mother and father are deceased, and you inherited a small chain of auto-body shops, which you ran into the ground before the age of twenty-six." One by one, I undo the buttons of my black dress shirt before removing it and tossing it aside along with the tank top underneath. Both are dirty and will be burned. "That is you, no?"

"Yes." Garbled, he winces and whimpers while pressing a hand against the side Isaac struck. Tears gather and fall from those swollen-shut eyes while the act of unintentionally biting his lips causes another small rush of blood to drip down his chin.

Nodding, I crane my head from side to side. Shake my arms out. "And do you personally know the man who just spoke?"

"I-I do." Pain is written across his features. Talking is torture.

"Tell me his name?"

"Alfred Castillo."

His partner cries out an *I don't know him* again, but I hold up a single finger, cutting him off without looking away. My focus is on the *brains* of this idiocy.

"How long have you been working together?" At my question, Herbert mumbles something which earns him another kick, this one sending him face-first into the floor. "Answer me."

"*Fucking shit.*" His head bounces off the harsh steel ground, creating another wound, this time to his forehead. "Please stop."

"Then speak clearly. How. Long?"

"A-A year. I-I lost my job with the city toward the tail end of the pandemic."

"And how many people have you robbed, Herbert?" I hum, scratching at my short beard. "How valuable are you?"

"Successfully?" he asks, while this time Alfred makes a guttural sound of protest from the back of his throat. Same sentiment, to discourage the little snitch from speaking, and my eyes flick to him. I almost chuckle at the sight that greets me. The guard who'd been keeping time a few minutes prior is now standing behind Alfred while the latter is gagged by a piece of blood-soaked material. A piece of *his* shirt; that's called initiative and I approve of the gesture, nodding at the guard before turning my head toward a crying Herbert.

"Finish."

"Only one was successful."

That I already knew, but the victim was well hidden. My hackers haven't found the trace yet; I know everything but the name of who's pulling the strings and their end game.

"Who did you rob?" He hesitates for a moment, and I narrow my eyes. Tilt my head to the side. "Five, four…three—"

"Celia Armas."

Liliana's mother. *My* little rebel's mother who's currently traveling through Europe with a group of girlfriends celebrating the anniversary of the dissolution of her marriage. Armas Sr. is a difficult man to deal with—at times can be overbearing—but he doesn't try to pull rank with me.

Never has been able to.

Not even when I was a teenager, and more importantly, he loves his daughter. Both his children *and* ex-wife are his world, even if the latter divorced him. *Do they know about the break-in, though?*

"So this is personal? You're mad at Mayor Armas?"

"Not me. I worked as a clerk of the courts." A lie that ends with a hiss of pain. He worked in corrections along with Alfred, and that's how they managed to get criminal connections. "After the business tanked, I became a Dade County employee. Was there for a few years before I was let go unjustly."

"Are you sure about that?"

"Yes. I'd never lie."

"And what did you take?" I'm forcing back the need to slit his throat or maybe empty a clip inside his chest. Because if I was angry before, this incinerates any rationality I have left. No one touches her family: mother, brother—her politician father with self-righteous tendencies that oftentimes leads him down the wrong path. His greed for *more* blinds him, but it's her love for them *all* that protects them. "Answer me."

"A safety deposit box from the Allura condominium." Struggling through each word, he pushes himself up and into a kneeling position, hands held up in supplication. They tremble, as does the rest of him. "That's all I was hired to take. I swear it."

"How long ago was this?"

"Two months ago. We made sure no one was inside."

Before Liliana moved in. The *could've been* in Herbert's answer incinerates my blood—rationality—and my next question is grit out slowly. "Who ordered the hit?"

"I don't know."

"Now really isn't the time to test my patience, Mr. Mullaney." Before I'm done speaking, Isaac's beside him, ready to strike again, but stops at the shake of my head. Instead, I quickly glance at Alfred, and he understands the silent request.

Between him and the other guard, they drag Alfred over—fighting and thrashing—and force him to stand a few feet from his beaten friend. That's where he now cries and, with a gagged mouth, watches. Has a front-row view of what I will do to him at some point unless he can change my mind.

Because the name Celia Armas changed everything.

Liliana, her daughter, controls me.

One will die. One will live.

"Asking too many questions can get you killed in this business. I'm only given the target's name, the item description for pickup, and then payment after it's handed over." As Herbert speaks, the scent of piss reaches my nostrils and I find a puddle growing beneath his body. It mixes with the blood already staining my floor while reaching his friend's feet, soaking the bare skin and bottom of his pants. "I'll give you everything…the money, too, if that's what you need. Just let me leave."

"You didn't deliver the safe?"

"No. The customer paid, but then told me to hold on to it."

"Male or female?"

"Male."

"Thank you for your cooperation." Before his next inhale, I pull out my favorite butterfly knife from my back pocket and flick it, then my wrist. The sharp blade embeds into Herbert's forehead. He falls back immediately; it doesn't go in deep enough to kill, but I remedy that by walking over as he screams from his position on the floor and stomping on the pearl-finish handle.

There's a quick squelch and a little resistance because of his skull, but then all struggling ceases. His chest no longer rises. His eyes stare blankly at me as I stand to my full height.

Herbert Mullaney was useless to me and untrustworthy, but his friend can be subjugated. Alfred's a spineless cunt, but a good father from the intel I've gathered. If nothing else, he'll do what I ask to protect his children and their mother from having to bury him.

Within the span of a heartbeat, a horror-filled sound fills the space and it's raw, full of so much fear and pain that I smile. Even behind the gag, Alfred's fighting to be heard. To plead with me.

"Remove the rag," I say, not turning around to face them. There's movement behind me as one of my two employees does what I ask, and a second later, I hear a low prayer. A pathetic sob. "Speak up."

"Please don't kill me. I-I'm sorry…I'll do whatever you want."

"What could you possibly do for me?" This is a question I already know the answer to, but I'd like to think the idiot before me understands what led him here. The dead body sold him out to save his own flesh. "Convince me."

"I know where Herbert keeps the customer database."

"And…?"

"Mrs. Armas's belongings will be returned."

"Not enough, Mr. Castillo. Those are items I can retrieve myself." Bending, I grip the handle of my knife and with one sharp tug, yank it from the deceased asshole dirtying my floor. Blood drips from the sharp blade, and I stare at it for a few seconds before sliding my finger through the remaining wetness. "But there is something you can do for me."

"Anything. Anything you want."

"Bring me the head of the snake, and I'll forgive this debt. Can you do that?" As I give him my terms, I watch through a mirror across from me as Isaac pulls out the manila envelope we'd prepared for something else but will work now just the same. It'd been folded in half, the contents inside a mere three pages, and then I hear the muted thud as he slams it against Alfred's chest along with a loaded Glock, safety in place. *That had to hurt.* "Do this, and I'll let you walk away. Betray me, and I'll kill you in front of everyone you love."

"He's not in Florida."

"Then find him."

"Can I have protection for my family?" At his question, I turn around. There are tears running down his mutilated cheek while a sob builds in his chest. Neither moves me. "They're innocent in all of this."

This is a self-inflicted problem his idiocy helped create.

Never attack a predator without leaving it dead because the bite in retaliation will kill.

"No one will touch them." A promise made because hurting innocents isn't something I do. Liliana would shoot me herself for it. Would be disappointed in me. *My rebel is a feisty one.* Walking over, I tower over his shuddering frame and silently slide my blood-stained thumb across his forehead, marking him with his associate's blood sealing our deal. "You have one week to bring me the person who ordered the thefts. Not a second more."

Without waiting for a response, I turn and walk toward my private elevator with Isaac a few steps behind. And right before the metal doors close, I pull out my gun and set off one shot. It rips through the air and digs into the neck of the informant—the one guard who never helped or moved during the entire interrogation—as they bought him to give them a layout of my ship.

His death serves two purposes:

Never betray me. Nothing stays hidden for long.

The rest of my crew will handle the cadaver and Mr. Castillo. Some will guide a nervous Alfred toward the empty cell where he'll spend the rest of the night before getting off my ship at the next port, while the cleaners will wash and sanitize the mess after releasing Herbert out to sea where nature will run its course.

The ride up to my private quarters is short, as is my patience; I need to see her. Make sure she's safe.

Isaac stays outside of my office after I enter, and I'm in front of my desk within a few strides. I'm quick to scan my thumb on the keyboard that pulls up the feed from her mother's condo, finding her immediately. She's in her bedroom asleep and oblivious. All warm and sweet and mine; a decadent bundle curled up under a soft blanket while her dark hair creates a halo around her.

My world: one whose peace has been threatened.

My queen: she will always come first.

Never taking my eyes off the screen, I say her brother's name out loud and a second later, the line rings twice and then clicks.

"Micah, it's—"

"We have a fucking problem."

Chapter 2
LILIANA

"**...A**re you even listening to me, Liliana? Mr. Royce demanded those files to be ready by—"

The answer to her question this Monday morning is a resounding no. Not really, as the bits and pieces of Beverly's annoying chatter make no sense to me. *His* secretary's words are muddled in the background, buried beneath the rising beat of my heart and the small gasp that escapes me as the ding of the elevator reverberates throughout the top floor of his cruise line headquarters.

No one outside of those with immediate access is allowed here and two of us are standing in my office, though my clearance is unlimited while hers is monitored. Which means...

Micah Royce is here.

Back after a few days out at sea monitoring the newest ship's first voyage; to me, his absence is always excruciating. I'm attuned to even the smallest vibration when it comes to this man. Affected by my boss—his mere presence—when he sees me as nothing more than a family friend.

To him, I'm his best friend's little sister.

To me, he's a powerful force that never fails to weaken my knees and ruin my panties.

In his presence, I'm always left wanting more…

Of his time. His touch. His everything.

Taking in a deep breath, I let it out slowly while pushing away a memory that torments my every nerve ending. A teasing shackle that brings goosebumps to my skin while the woman in front of me remains oblivious to my torture.

Micah kissed me once. On my eighteenth birthday while—

"Really, Liliana? Where is your head today!" Beverly hisses, her hand waving in front of my face while I simply blink twice from behind my desk. Once again, I don't answer her, but I do raise a brow at the sharp tone. We're not friends, much less have anything to do with each other, yet she's here ruining my morning routine.

Since the day I began at his company, under the guise of garnering work experience as part of my final grade last semester, I've come in and brewed our coffee before setting up his day. For months now, his daily meetings and calls with every cruise director setting sail—going over last-minute changes and finalizing approvals —are all coordinated by me, unbeknownst to him.

I choose the day each department hands over its weekly reports.

I make the necessary arrangements for food deliveries that are delayed or sent back due to not meeting quality standards.

I make sure nothing with peanuts or a derivative comes within a hundred feet of him.

Not this secretary, who's been here slightly longer than me yet doesn't have a clue about his needs. Beverly's good at taking all the credit, and for the most part, I'm okay with that, yet today she's trying to harass me out of panic.

However, she's meeting a defiant wall while trying to shift the blame for a file that up until last night was still on her desk. I'm not a pushover—I do what I do for him—and don't take kindly to her attitude. This is my downtime she's encroaching on. My daily allotted reprieve where I catch my breath and then recite a set of vows that carry no real weight to them.

Because moving on from this unrequited obsession is impossible when he destroys my paper-thin walls each morning at eight a.m. sharp with nothing more than a simple: *Buenos Dias.*

I'm that easy. A slave to my un-satiated needs.

Two mere words spoken in my family's native tongue, and I crumble like my favorite cookie.

Maybe I should give online dating an honest try.

The blasphemous thought immediately leaves a bitter taste in my mouth. It's an impossibility, and for reasons beyond my comprehension, Micah's all I've ever been able to see.

No man calls my attention. No one sets my blood on fire with a simple smile.

"Why are you here, Beverly?" My tone is curt, yet polite enough that she doesn't pick up on my annoyance. How distracted I am because he's closer now, having bypassed his private waiting area and now walking toward my office—one of the two on this floor. "That isn't my department and you know it. I'm not the head of marketing."

"No. Just…cyber analysis, was it?"

"Cybersecurity. What's your point?"

"You don't belong up here."

"And you do?" I ask while reaching for my cup of coffee. The mug is still warm and feels good against my always-cold fingers. And while Beverly becomes red in the face and her expression shows her true bitterness, I take a generous sip of my hazelnut *nectar of the gods* beverage with a smile.

For a few seconds after, I take her in while letting the caffeine perk me up.

She's a beautiful woman; I can admit that. With straight copper hair, stark green eyes, and full lips, her face draws attention, but the moment she opens her mouth, the allure vanishes. Sure, there's a great body attached, but vanity can only get you but so far when there's no real substance.

There's also one thing I have that she doesn't, and I know it infuriates her.

I have a desk. An entire office on this floor.

Beverly, and the ones before her, have all been relegated to the two levels directly below where I sit. That's the assistant's domain— the CEO's and the head of every department's for that matter— something she hates. In this company, every superior holds an office outside of their designated unit, which makes it a much more enjoyable atmosphere for their team to flourish.

It was one of Micah's first changes after taking over as CEO after his father stepped down.

Helps with productivity—works for everyone *but* his personal assistant. I've heard Beverly's complaints. Took the snide remarks with a grain of salt in the past, but today's just not the day to test my patience.

The insulting retort sits on my tongue, but then I stop. This is what she wants.

Is she hoping Micah catches me going off on her? To embarrass me?

"What is it that you actually do here, Lola?" Condescension drips from her every word while she gets my name wrong on purpose, but I don't take the bait. Instead, I shift my attention to his heavier footfalls, something she's oblivious to for someone so set on creating a scene. *Or maybe she is aware? Maybe she'll cry on cue and accuse me of stealing the report?* "You're a part of this company, and yet, I never see you do more than type away at your screen or make his coffee. Everyone else busts their asses—"

"Is that what bothers you?" I cock my head to the side while placing my near-empty cup down. On the outside, I appear calm, yet inside it's a turbulent wave—two opposing emotions rattling my cage. She is a nuisance, and he is my weakness. "Are you upset that Mr. Royce prefers my abilities to your lacking ones?"

"Yet I get the praise."

"Do you really? Or is that what you tell yourself?" It takes everything in me to keep my expression neutral, but I do, no matter how close I am to my limit. Moreover, the closer he gets, the harder it becomes to fight against the havoc each Italian-shoed step creates in me. My core clenches at nothing and my clit throbs, needing something I've yet to discover while Beverly glares at me.

Because his effect is a living, breathing pulse inside of me. An electrical current that comes to life when the man I love is near, or worse, when the first hint of his scent infiltrates my senses like it is right now.

He's a note of citrus with a touch of bourbon on a warm night.

He's smoky and earthy and everything that sets my skin ablaze.

"Please." The scoff drips with disdain. Arrogance. "We all know you got this job because your brother—"

"Finish that sentence, Ms. Mills. I dare you." Micah's deep timbre is calm as he steps just inside my office, yet the tinge of ire is unmistakable. It's hypnotic, really. His anger permeates the air surrounding him while his sharp jaw clenches and those azure eyes darken the moment they set on mine.

A gaze that softens for a brief moment as it skates along my skin, from my temple to my lips and then lower, to the top of my blouse before retaking my stare. For me, it feels as though his fingers have traced a map along my skin, yet I know better...

Micah doesn't see me as anything more than a friend.

He's simply protective of those he cares about.

Will that ever not sting?

And while he stands there like a god among men leaning against my doorframe, I exhale slowly while taking him in. From his impeccably cut Dior suit in a charcoal tone, tailor-made to fit his six foot four frame, to his white dress shirt sans tie with the first two buttons undone—the man is sinful. There's also a small pocket square that I recognize and my heart flutters, loving the touch of me on him.

I bought this one for him last Christmas from a local designer that I'm a fan of; a constellation-themed silk handkerchief in black and white with his initials in the right bottom corner. My lips tug a bit at the sight, but I remain outwardly calm while pleasure fills me.

Lower, I find his tattoos peeking out from the cuffs. The stark nautical artwork is beautiful and a piece I'm envious of as he clenches his fist against his right thigh. Thighs that are encased in slim-cut trousers; they mold and enhance, and I swallow hard at the large bulge that's ever-present.

My entire being reacts. Warms. Yet with as much aloofness as I can muster, I flick my eyes to my now-cool mug and grab it, ignoring them while willing my heart to relax.

I take a few small sips, wishing I could get up and make a new coffee. Regroup far from him.

Dear Lord. Can you please help a girl out?

"Mr. Royce, I'm—" Beverly gasps, spinning around to face him, but that's as far as she gets.

His head shakes and a single finger is held up, gaze still on me. Can feel the weight of it. "Is this how she always speaks to you, Liliana?" She bristles at that, something he also notices as his eyes switch from her to me. Just as I do to them. Can't help but take a look. My attention pings back and forth as the atmosphere inside my office becomes almost unbearable beneath the tension. His brows furrow and his jaw ticks, a rigidness that doesn't sit well with me, and all I want to do is run my fingers across Micah's skin—smooth out the strain there. "Do you have a problem with my question? Or is it Ms. Armas you dislike? Explain yourself."

Beverly relaxes her stance and smiles softly, trying to appear demure. "Mr. Royce, you've misunderstood me. Liliana and I work very well together—"

"You shouldn't be around her at all." Stepping fully into the room, he comes around my desk and stands to my right. It's a position that shows loyalty to me and I'm both aroused and surprised, the latter of which because we keep our ties outside of the office just that…outside.

Here, I'm an employee. I'm not someone who's had dinner with his mom and dad or celebrated holidays together as our families tend to do. Even after my parents divorced, it never changed. Our interactions have always been the same: close and panty-destroying.

"Mr. Royce, I don't understand…" she trails off, eyes shifting and pleading with me for help. How? I have no clue. Not that I'm inclined to either way, especially after her attitude just a short while ago. "My relationship with Lili—"

"Why does someone who works in my IT department have to help you with anything outside of malfunctioning equipment or security issues?" Micah places a hand on my shoulder and gives a short squeeze, causing a shiver to run through me. Not that he calls me out on it. Instead, I'm greeted by the tap of two fingers over the same spot and a low hum I find utterly sexy. "I'm waiting for your explanation."

"She's gracious and helps—"

"I know she is. More than she should be." Micah's tone comes out cold. Biting, almost. But more than that, his interjection causes my head to snap in his direction, finding him already looking at me. There's a knowing look in place. A raised brow to match the challenging expression. *He knows.* "Did you really think I wasn't aware of Liliana organizing my schedule? That my office doesn't have cameras?"

Micah holds me captive for a few more seconds until satisfied, and then deems her worthy of attention. His question is biting—tinged with anger—while the color drains from her face. While I bite my bottom lip, not knowing how to feel about any of this.

Every time I'm in his office, I run my fingers across his things. I sit in his chair with my eyes closed while taking in his intoxicating scent, a unique pheromone that fills every square inch of that room.

I've whimpered with need; one I don't satiate as I've been saving myself for him.

Hoping. Dreaming. Wanting someone who will never see me that way.

Moreover, neither of us answer him. The seconds tick by and the longer he waits, I see the anger shift and grow, but it's not directed at me. *Has he ever been mad at me? Truly mad?*

The answer is no. Not once.

And as if he knows I'm about to test that theory by asking everyone to take a moment and breathe, Micah puts a little pressure on my shoulder. His hand keeps me in place.

"Sir, I…" Beverly says then, the sound coming out croaky, and she pauses to clear her throat. Her hands are also shaky, twitching at her sides, and while with anyone else I'd feel bad, for her I'm unmoved. Not twenty minutes ago, I was being scolded and used as a scapegoat and now, she looks to me for help. Stupidly, and with glistening eyes, she also takes a few steps in his direction while ignoring the irate expression on his face. "Sir…Micah, we're all—"

"It's Mr. Royce to you, and there's no *we* here. Know your place." Tone dry and harsh, I shiver at it, and he's quick to rub his thumb across my shoulder blade. He hasn't stopped touching me in one way or another. Even if it is all innocent, Micah is killing me. Teasing me.

"Of course, Mr. Royce. My apologies." Looking at me, Beverly smiles and lowers her head a tiny bit as if to appear apologetic. Contrite. "Being co-workers and a tight-knit unit, I saw no harm when Liliana asked me to let her make arrangements for you. It's my notes and files and methods she uses to keep your day moving smoothly, as I'd do. But if that is a problem, I promise it won't happen again."

"I thought you said she *helps* you."

"She does. There's so much work—"

"So what you're saying is you can't handle your job?"

"N-No. Of course not," she quickly stammers, eyes wide with panic. "I love my job."

"So you think you're ready for any challenge? Can run any department as she has?"

"Without a single doubt, Mr. Royce." Beverly's prompt response almost makes me laugh; she walked into that set-up without any lubrication. Because the one thing I know about Micah —as a teen and now as a man—is he doesn't appreciate lying. He'll force the truth out of you one way or another. "I'm confident in my—"

"Good. Then tomorrow morning you'll be reporting to Weber in accounting."

"What?"

"Congratulation, Ms. Mills. He's your new boss."

"I-I don't understand. I'm your secretary and—"

"And this is my company, Ms. Mills." Giving my shoulder a final squeeze, Micah walks back to the entrance and points toward the elevator. "Clear your desk, and don't you ever speak to one of my employees like that again. This is your only warning, Beverly. Step a single toe out of line again, and I won't hesitate to fire you." Her lips drop open; she wants to say something, but at the shake of his head, Beverly lowers hers and walks away.

Neither of us speaks until she's inside the elevator and the doors ding, signaling they're closed. Instead, I watch his reaction and fall in love with the crooked smile he turns and gives me once we're alone again.

It's my smirk. The one he's gifted me since we met.

"Always in trouble, little Rebel."

"Not my fault this time. I've been a saint here, Micah."

"Is that so?" At my nod, he rubs his jaw and my thighs clench of their own accord. My entire being throbs with the simple act. There's also a little darkening of his eyes as if his thoughts mimic my own, but I know that's wishful thinking on my part. "Doesn't sound like fun."

"It's been hard to play nice."

"Then let's shake things up a bit, Ms. Armas. I have a proposition for you."

Chapter 3
LILIANA

"*I have a proposition for you.*"

"As long as it doesn't leave any visible marks." Without conscious thought, the retort slips past my lips, and embarrassment blooms from the apple of my cheeks to the top of my breasts. Heat ripples across my skin, leaving me flushed and sensitive, unable to control my body's reaction to his nearness—to shake off the effects his mere presence creates.

Because rationality fails me time and time again, and in its place, I'm left simpering while my traitorous body just wants to please him.

Anything he wants. Anytime.

Jesus Christ, Liliana. Get it together. A chastisement a little too late as I struggle to meet his gaze, one that penetrates every wall I try to erect in his name. Instead, I'm left with no choice but to stand and walk out of the room with my coffee mug in hand, pretending to need another fix. I'm not running away per se, but trying and failing to create distance between us so I can think clearly. But instead of letting me shake off his hold, I'm followed by his heavy-set footsteps into our private mini kitchen.

He's never more than a few steps from me. His six-foot-four frame dwarfs mine.

"That sounds like a dare, Rebel." Amusement drips from his tone and against my better judgment, I look up, losing myself in his azure eyes. There's mirth there, but even headier is this hint of dark promise that I don't quite understand. *Has to be the lighting. Second time today.* "Are you challenging your boss?"

And if I was? What would you do about it? The retort sits on the tip of my tongue, which I bite back, along with the threat of my thighs clenching. Instead, I shrug and pretend this is all a joke. Messing around with a good friend while a grin that matches his tugs at my lips. "Not a threat. More like a warning."

"Is that so? Should I be afraid, Liliana?"

"Positively terrified." And to add to my dramatics, I snap my teeth at him before placing a new pod in the coffee machine. I'm on autopilot at this point, just like breathing, but the racing of my heart tells a different story. As does the small shake in my hands; I pretend they're cold and rub my palms together to complete the act. "I'm not cut out for the secretary life, Micah. Will do just about anything to avoid being your gopher."

He's not offended in the least. If anything, Micah's holding back a laugh. "I'm not that bad, Rebel."

"Says you." While the machine percolates, I move to the sink and rinse my mug before starting my ritual. I'm not one for over-the-top coffee drinks, but there are two staples I can't do without: my sweet cold foam and my hazelnut creamer. Grabbing the ingredients for both while trying my best to ignore his body heat—how close to me he stands—I grab a second mug for him. Each of the ones here has a matching counterpart, and if he notices the *his* and *hers* theme I've developed, Micah doesn't say a word. Pouring a bit of heavy whipping cream and a touch of 2% milk into my frothing mini-pitcher, I turn to reach for the vanilla syrup but he already has it in his hand, placing it on the countertop beside me. "Thanks."

"Make mine a bit stronger today. I had a long night."

"Sure. Double or triple shot?" Not that I wait for his answer as a sharp pang of fury—jealousy—nearly robs me of breath, but I don't make a sound. I don't turn and look at him while I make enough for both cups and then prepare his and mine however I see fit. It's the best thing to do at the moment; concentrate and pretend that he wasn't with someone last night.

He's never mentioned anyone before. Who is—

"I had a small incident aboard the ship last night that delayed my return."

"I'm sorry. What?"

"Look at me," Micah says, tone softer yet a bit deeper. Like smooth whiskey or a rich piece of chocolate, and I do as he asks without a second of hesitation. Blue eyes on hazel, and I can't so much as breathe when he lifts a hand and pushes a stray piece of hair behind my ear. "We had an altercation after an attempted robbery in my stateroom. Everyone is safe. Those involved were caught and *dealt with*. I promise."

"Everything's fine?" I'm filled with a different kind of apprehension now. Without pause, I abandon our drinks and check him for any place he could've been hurt. I run my fingers gingerly up his arms to his shoulders and then stroke down his sides to his ribs. There's no flinching or anything that indicates a gauze or dressing, but I *am* met with firm muscles beneath the expensive cut of his suit.

His muscles twitch beneath my touch, and yet he doesn't pull away. If anything, he takes a single step closer. "Yes, Rebel."

"Swear it." My open palm rests against his right pectoral while our eyes meet once again. I know I'm blushing and that goosebumps have spread across my skin at our proximity, but the worry over anything happening to him outweighs my desire to hide the way my nipples pebble beneath my beaded lace demi-bra with a bow at the center. The thin fabric of my blouse doesn't help either, not that he looks.

Those heady blues stay on mine. "I'd never lie to you. You can always trust me."

And I do. He's never given me a single reason to doubt or question him, not even when he disappears from time to time without an explanation. He'd be gone for a few weeks at a time, come back, and then return to wherever he went, and not even Lionel knows much.

Does he have someone? A thought my heart rejects almost as soon as it hits. My entire being does because he'd never hide that. Not from his family.

"I trust you, Micah. Always have."

"Good girl." The effect those words have on me is heady, but I hide behind the guise of stepping back and turning toward our cooling coffees. I push Micah's toward him before grabbing mine, and with a hum that quickly morphs into a low moan, I hide behind the first sweet sip while he watches my every move. It's moments like these that confuse and further ignite my hopes for him. Of there being an *us* someday. "You've always had an unhealthy obsession with caffeine..." his chuckle creates more warmth than my drink "... sometimes I think it's your first love."

"No. Not my first." I shrug, but keep my lips against the mug's rim while taking in the way the foam begins to disperse, mixing with the light tan drink. "But it's the most loyal relationship I've ever had."

"Who was your first love, Liliana?" It might be my imagination, but there's a hidden tinge of anger in his question. One that pulls my eyes to his. His expression is neutral, but the tick of his jaw is a sign of his displeasure, one I have an automatic compulsion to soothe. Moreover, in order not to pet him—stroke his chest—I wrap my fingers tighter around the ceramic cup. "Have you been keeping secrets, Liliana?"

"No." This comes out a bit shaky, but I clear my throat and smile. "All my love affairs are entangled with national brand products, a few coffee machines, and my collection of romance novels. No male attention...*yet*."

"Yet?" More at ease. His posture is a bit more relaxed.

"Yes. *Yet*." I might love Micah, but one day I want it all...

To have someone who is as head over heels for me as I am for them. To lose my virginity.

I want marriage and a home full of memories. Children that come from love and not duty.

"Hmmm." That's it. That's all he gives me before we hear the ding of the elevator, and I know it's the end of our conversation. His head gives a subtle tilt in the direction of the footsteps heading toward his office, the sound alerting me it's a male, yet his attention remains on me.

"Are you expecting someone?" I ask then, brows furrowing while *my* eyes do shift, trying to catch the visitor through the kitchen's entrance. We're towards the back end of this floor, but I still have a clear view of anyone heading toward Micah's door. My office is on the opposite wall and a little further up, hidden from this vantage point. "I didn't see any meetings on the itinerary. Your day is pretty clear."

"This one's off the books."

"With who?" Curiosity is a bitch, and I'm nosy. More so when it comes to him.

"Your brother."

"What's Lionel doing here? He's supposed to be out of town." Last week, he'd made arrangements with our father to visit Talla-hassee and attend a dinner with the governor tonight. They'd gone to discuss the plans and funds needed to rebuild an area affected by two hurricanes that swept through our city last year and created quite a mess for businesses and residents alike.

Our tropical beaches are a gold mine for those families who invested in Florida tourism then and now. Old money meets new ambition, and anything that isn't built with luxury in mind or set to preserve the art deco touch that's graced Miami Beach since the early 1930s is unacceptable. People come from all over the world to experience our shores, and the state loses millions in revenue when our hotels, clubs, and shorelines are empty.

"We have some business to discuss, but I do appreciate how proactive you are."

"Proactive? Or nosy?"

Raising his hand, Micah taps the bridge of my nose twice before sweeping his knuckles across my still-heated cheeks. A touch I ignore. Can't give myself false hope. "You're well acquainted with my schedule, Rebel. You'll be perfect."

"Perfect for what?" Not that he answers. Instead, Micah ignores the question while using the same hand to pick up his coffee and walk past me. Not that I let him reach the door, though. He's at the threshold when I can't help but blurt out the first thing that comes to mind. "I'm not going to run around in these heels."

At that, he pauses. His back muscles are a little stiff, but his head snaps in my direction and he looks at me from over his shoulder. His head dips and his darkening eyes flick down to my feet where they stay; I bought this pair a few weeks ago from an online boutique after a famous actress walked the red carpet wearing them.

They were simply stunning and with the perfect name to match: Harlot.

Black leather pumps with silver-toned hardware that's bold and edgy while the strap around the ankle is sexy. I'd never seen a footwear line like this before. Between their signature pointed toe and the metal heel, I was head over shoes in love with the Hardot brand.

I bought them without a second thought, and I've never been prouder of a purchase.

Or the one that followed. Especially with the way he continues to stare at them.

"You will."

"Will what, Mr. Royce?"

"Be under me, Ms. Armas."

"W-What—?"

"Starting this very second, you're my new secretary."

Chapter 4
MICAH

"You're in an awfully good mood for a man threatening to shoot me just a few hours ago," Lionel says from his seat across my desk, eyeing the cup of coffee I'd set down to my right. On his face, there's a smirk, the ever-present knowledge that I'm controlled by a woman I've yet to claim, and that hurting him would cause her distress.

Distress is a word that should never be associated with my glorious little rebel. Something he knows. My love for her gives the grinning asshole a small sense of comfort because she's happy and I've kept my promises. Liliana Armas is:

Protected.

Untouched.

Cared for.

Just a few more months, and she'll be everything but *pure.*

His eyes shift from me to the mug; a cocky smirk grows by the second because the cold foam, her signature preference, still sits atop this sweet concoction. Lionel knows I only drink this because she made it, and that by choice, I like my coffee black and unsweetened, but for her, I've always swallowed each sugary sip without complaint.

Only for her. I'd do anything she asks.

Sitting back, I narrow my eyes. "The offer still sits, Armas. Want to test it?"

He raises a brow, a challenge I will make him eat one day. "I could call my sister in here."

"And I'd kick your ass the second she steps outside this room."

Throwing his head back, my best friend laughs. It's loud and obnoxious with a snort or two mixed in—it's something he has in common with Liliana—but on her, I find the action adorable. Everything she does is nothing short of perfection. "If anyone else held the kind of obsession you have for her, I'd have them strung up by their balls while they watched me saw their dick off. Might even make them eat it afterward."

"But I'm not just anyone and you know it."

"I do." The earlier amusement dies, and in front of me now sits the groomed politician he was brought up to be. His father wanted him to follow in his footsteps. To start local and then state before making a bid for the White House. Yet what they all fail to see is a man who's ruthless—he's no one's puppet—and it's one of the reasons our friendship has lasted this long. We'd kill for those we love. Pushing his black hair back, Lionel's brown eyes, a few shades darker than his sister's, stare back. "It's why I've never forbidden this relationship. You'll be good for and to her."

"Her happiness is all that matters to me." At my words, he nods and opens his mouth to add something, which I find irrelevant—I continue before he can. "I've always respected her and our friendship. Up to a certain point I've been patient and understanding, but never mistake my affection for her as any form of compliance. I don't need your consent, Lionel, but appreciate it nonetheless because it'll make her happy to know you approve."

"You're an arrogant bastard, Royce, but that's why you have it. No one will protect and love her as you will."

"I'd also kill anyone that'd try."

"Speaking of killing...what happened on your ship?" There's a knock on the door seconds after his question, cutting our conversation short while the person on the other end doesn't wait for me to let them in. The door opens and my reason for breathing peeks her head in, long, dark waves sweeping across one shoulder while giving her brother a small grin.

Liliana steps inside with a tray full of pastries and another indulgent concoction, steam billowing from the top of the ceramic cup. Because she always makes him tea. Lionel, unlike his sister, has never been a fan of coffee, yet he does indulge in steeped leaves and dried fruit.

"I won't apologize for interrupting..." Liliana trails off, placing a silver tray down right on top of a manila folder with a partnership proposal from a local farming company. They're offering me a substantial discount compared to that of my current supplier while guaranteeing the same quality—fresh produce and fruits to cover every meal and snack we provide our guests.

Food is one of the biggest expenses for any cruise line, rivaled closely by alcohol.

"Sister."

"Big brother," she mimics his deep tone, lip twitching while I shift my eyes from her to the folder. My raised brow makes her smile just a little wider, straight white teeth embedded into her bottom lip to hold in a laugh. *Naughty girl.* The move was on purpose, but before I can admonish her, she's waving a hand between us. "I'm not interested in whatever this is, but Dahlia from human resources brought these as a gift for me. Her sister opened a shop inside Bayside Marketplace, and she wants me to give them a try. You know how much I love my pastelitos with guava and cream cheese."

"You could eat a box of those turnovers by yourself," Lionel snorts under his breath, shaking his head at her. More so when he goes to grab one, and his sister snatches it before he can. "Not nice, kid. I thought those were for us?"

"Says who? I'm sharing everything *but* those." The perplexed look on her face is genuine and I can't stop the laugh that bursts from me, causing the siblings to tilt their heads to the side simultaneously. One grumbling, while the other—the one that matters—rolls her eyes as if to say, *can you believe him?*

Motherfuck, I just want to bite her. Eat her.

From her pouty cherry lips down to that perky set of tits, then down to the sweetness between her luscious thighs, my teeth ache—my mouth waters from need. Just like my cock throbs beneath the cover of my ebony desk, pulsing in time with each rise and fall of her chest. Each jerk is bordering on painful pleasure, flesh digging into the teeth of my zipper while beads of pre-come slip from the swollen tip.

I've counted more than eight now. I feel each one as it rolls down the underside, teasing my skin with a soft caress that I imagine to be her tongue.

I'm torturing myself, but don't break.

Not yet.

I'll reap my reward soon enough.

Instead, I pick up my cup and take a large sip, letting the overly sweet concoction pull my attention away from the urge to ram my cock inside one of her tiny holes. Mouth, pussy, or ass…it doesn't matter which one; just being in her presence is near maddening, but the cloying aftertaste that lingers does enough that I appear normal to her.

Then again, my little Liliana doesn't know me any other way.

Not the killer. Not the asshole with a short temper.

Forcing the next swallow, I place the ceramic cup down. "Can I have one, Rebel?"

"One what?" There's a small hitch in her breath while those hazel eyes stare at my mouth.

"A guava and cream cheese turnover." My tone comes out gruffer than I intend, yet it has a delicious effect on her. At once, a touch of pink sweeps across the apple of her cheeks while goosebumps rise across her flesh. Then, there's a small shiver she tries hard to suppress and fails at doing so.

Each reaction makes me feel like a motherfucking king. Like her god.

"Yes."

"Yes what, Ms. Armas?"

"You can have them all." Her tone is sweet, yet sultry. *My perfection.*

"Good girl." An incredulous cough comes from her brother, but I pay him no heed and grab three pastries, placing them atop one of the two small plates found on the left corner of the large tray. "I'll reward my new secretary with her favorite lunch today."

"Okay." Still in a little bit of a trance, she answers, but then snaps out of it when her brother nudges her arm. The push isn't subtle and her beautiful eyes snap to him, narrowing while the other Armas sibling picks up a Cuban meat-filled turnover this time. "Rude, Lionel."

"That's what big brothers are for."

"To be a pain in the ass?"

"To help you not—"

"Leave my employee alone, Armas. She's a busy woman with a new title and a demanding boss breathing down her neck." I add in a wink at the end, my gaze always on her, and I'm glad because I catch the quick flash of annoyance in her features. The slight tightening of her eyes disappears on her next blink. "Rebel, what—"

"What do you mean she has a new title?" Lionel's tone is also off, drier than a moment ago as he cuts me off.

Breathing in deep, I let the interruption go. Remind myself that he can be an idiot at times. "She's my new assistant."

"What happened to Beverly? Are you finally sending her…" Her brother trails off at the look I give him, choosing to zip it and not incur my anger. I've given a lot of concessions to this family when it comes to her—I've been patient and know that putting a bullet into his head would devastate her—but I'll never accept anyone questioning my reasoning outside of Liliana.

If she asks, I'll gladly explain.

If she refuses, I'll just have to convince her.

"Problem with that?"

"Wait. You were serious?" We speak in unison, but it's the change in her tone I'm focused on. Her words are concise but low, yet to me, it's as if she's screamed them from the top of her lungs.

She isn't happy with me. *No, baby.*

Pushing my chair back, I walk around to where the siblings sit and take ahold of her wrist. She gives me a perplexed look but doesn't pull away, nor does she stop me when I tug her out of the room.

Her brother does call my name, but I pay him no mind.

Anything outside of her complete contentment is unacceptable.

I'm firm in my strides but careful enough that she never teeters in those ridiculously sexy heels. Heels that make her legs seem longer, wrap around her dainty feet in a sinful way and make me want to feel the metal dig into my skin. I want to fuck her for the first time, take her virginity while she wears them.

First. Second. A full night of those spikes and leather rubbing against my sides and back.

Soon. Just a little longer.

Not stopping until we reach her light and feminine office, I bring us inside and quickly shut the door. It closes with a gentle thud, nothing more than a low sound a second before her back meets the sleek, white acrylic panel a second later.

I'm towering over her as my chest expands on a ragged breath.

I'm taking her in from this position, fighting back the desire to taste her as she waits for an explanation.

On why I brought us here. On why I need her as my secretary. Or maybe she thinks I'll demand her compliance as I do with everyone else at this company, but never with her.

She has no idea she controls me.

We're not touching outside of my grip on her wrist, and even that, I keep gentle while sweeping my thumb across her pulse point. "Talk to me, sweetheart. What's wrong?"

"I can't be your secretary, Micah," she answers quickly, her doe-eyes looking at me with nothing but trust in them. There's also a bit of heat, her own desires coming through. It's there in the way she catches her lip between her teeth, how her chest rises and falls with each deep breath, and how those mouthwatering nipples tighten as they press against the thin fabric of her blouse. "It's not what we agreed upon."

Instead of responding, though, I leaned down and kiss the tip of her nose—breathe in deep and fill my lungs with her intoxicating cupcake scent while fighting back the urge to lick her cheek. Her neck. To swipe my tongue across her plump lips before claiming them as mine.

I do none of those things—keeping my hunger in check—but I do lift the hand not holding her wrist and cup the back of her neck. My hold is possessive, a tenth of the need causing my cock to painfully throb, and I smile down at her. "Why?"

"Because I'm part of your IT department."

"I'm aware. Your schooling has always been a priority to me." I caress the soft skin underneath each fingertip. Each touch is meant to soothe her. "However, that doesn't answer the why?"

Liliana's tongue peeks out then from between her plump lips and glides across the bottom one. The action is innocent; I don't believe she's aware of just how sexy it is. "Then you must understand that I like my arrangement here as is. This will interfere with my internship; I need these logged hours for my final grade this semester."

"It won't. I promise."

"Micah, please find someone else. I'm not—"

"I need someone I can trust, Liliana." Bending my knees a bit, I lower my body just enough that my forehead lays on hers. Keep our eyes locked. "After the attempted theft on the ship, knowing it was one of my employees that sold the company out, I'm concerned. You're the only one that I—"

"Okay." She breathes out. No hesitation.

"Just like that?"

"Yup. You need me, and I'm here."

"Thank you, love."

The term of endearment slips from me, but Liliana doesn't call me out on it. Instead, she leans up and kisses my cheek before pushing me back and I let her, releasing my hold on her neck. For a few seconds, we stare at each other and don't move. Just follow the other's breathing patterns, the tension between us palpable—my muscles twitch and I'm about to pull her close once again when her desk phone rings.

It breaks the moment. Forces a shuddering breath from her chest, and I'm strong enough to walk away from the temptation. One of the last times I'll ever do this again. Our time is coming.

Soon, baby. Moreover, I'm almost at the door when I change my mind and look at her over my shoulder. "Take the rest of the day off. You'll start tomorrow."

"Who's going to help you here? Plus, I have to meet up with Jeremy for our weekly—"

"No," I interrupt and her eyes narrow. Lips purse. "That can wait until next week."

"What do you mean *no*, Micah? He's not just your employee, Jeremy's my TA and I need to show my work for the week and proof of logged hours." Exasperated, she huffs. Folds her arms across her chest, and the way it pushes her tits together is simply beautiful. "I'm so close to graduating and can't afford to slip. That, and I'm needing a bit of help picking the basis of my final project."

"Relax, sweetheart. You won't fall behind; I won't let that happen."

"But, Micah—"

"But nothing, Rebel. Be a good girl for me and go home." From over my shoulder, I send her a wink while swiping my tongue across my bottom lip. Her eyes follow the move, eyes darkening just a tiny bit, and it takes everything in me not to stride back inside and kiss the ever-loving fuck out of her. "And expect a treat from me tonight. It'll be there at six."

Chapter 5
MICAH

"I'm not even going to ask."

"Good. You shouldn't," I answer her brother, retaking my seat behind my desk while raising a brow at the crumbs on his shirt and the powdered sugar on his fingers. He's just as bad as my rebel, having left nothing on the tray but was smart enough not to touch the ones I'd left on a plate for myself. "And I won't either. Plausible deniability."

"Best decision of your life." Lionel's shrug is nonchalant, but those words are quickly followed by a tightening around his eyes, his lips in a straight line. Then, there's the way his posture becomes stiff —a nervous tick he's never exuded before also starts in his leg. It bounces rapidly, while the fingers of his right hand tap an off-rhythm on his knee.

Tap. Tap. Tap. Tap.

I'd never seen him this way before. Something's wrong.

"Tell me." My tone is hard. Tinged with ire; an explosion of dark promise grows within me with each second that ticks on the clock. "What the fuck is going on, Armas?"

"Is she in danger, Micah?"

"Is that a question, or am I missing something here?" Leaning forward, I place both hands down flat on my dark-colored desk. "Explain."

This entire space is the antithesis of my future wife's office. Where hers is light and what she calls *boss babe* chic, mine is dark woods and black-paneled walls with gold trim throughout. From the flooring to the furniture, everything within is a play on my favorite color: black. The only artificial light source in this room comes from a chandelier she chose after I took over for my father, claiming to hate the previous one, while the floor-to-ceiling windows on the right side take care of the daylight hours.

We're a Yin and Yang.

Darkness and light.

"Micah, it's more complicated—"

"I won't ask again. What. Is. Going. On?"

Lionel exhales roughly while looking away, rubbing a harsh hand down his face and in these last few minutes, he's changed. Gone is the relaxed yet strong man with political ambitions I know.

This isn't the same man who entered my office gloating in his amusement—the knowledge that I'm held by a set of vows I'd only break for one reason: her safety.

The kind his answer could present.

"I'm asking because if she were, you'd already know."

"I would." No point in hiding it. He knows I keep track of her movements. "But so would you."

"At the moment, she's not under direct threat, but I'm worried,

Micah. Things aren't as clean as my father wants them to appear."
Eyes so much like his sister's meet mine again. They show real
worry. A hint of fear. "He pissed someone off."

"Is that why your mother's condo was robbed? Why two men
were hired to take her safety deposit box?" I ask, but it comes across
as a clear accusation. At the moment, I'm holding myself back from
standing and wrapping a hand around his throat. From going after
my rebel's father; I'll deal with him after.

Her safety comes first.

Nothing matters more than that.

That's something her brother knows and I give him credit for;
Lionel keeps his emotions under control for the most part. Very little
reaction, but a wave of anger that matches my own comes through
loud and clear when you're good at reading people. His concern is
replaced by ire, even if it's contained. It's there in the way his hands
clench—the flaring of his nostrils and the slight tick of his jaw as his
teeth grind.

Because everyone has a tell, and emotional displays don't differ
that much from one person to the next when you know what you're
looking for. It's why liars get caught. Why happiness and anger,
extreme opposites on the spectrum, hold one thing in common: facial
expressions.

Be it the tightness around the eyes or a curl of the lips, no one
can stop these twitches from happening. Even the most even-keeled
have a moment of weakness before they return to their stoic
demeanors.

"When?" One word, but it's spit out through clenched teeth.

"Do Alfred Castillo and Herbert Mullaney ring any bells?"

"No. Who the fuck are they?"

"They were caught on my ship. Two low-level thieves with high
aspirations and idiotic tendencies." Standing from my seat, I push
my chair back and walk around the desk—away from him and the
desire to react violently. There's a mini bar near the opposite wall
and I make my way over, grabbing two glasses from the next shelf

down. Like me, Lionel drinks whiskey and I pour us each a couple of fingers' worth. "Caught one in my vault and the other on a Jet Ski heading toward the lowest hydraulic exit. He'd taken Liliana's ring and a hard drive—they were hired by the same people who struck against your mother."

"Son of a bitch." It's loud, as is the knocking back of his seat. The action is hard enough it nearly slams into the wall, but Lionel is lucky it doesn't. Because of this, I don't say anything about the mistreatment of my furniture, giving him this reprieve while holding out his drink. He knows this and gives me a nod, following me a second later by knocking back his own drink as I pour myself a second.

Had he alerted Liliana to something being wrong…

"I'm not going to give you a warning."

"I know." Holding out his glass, he tips it and I pour. This one we don't drink from, holding them as the sound of a ship leaving the dock filters through the thick glass. My building sits close to the main port, and day in and day out, the sound of horns, engines, and heavy machinery has become a background playlist. One that I tune out for the most part, but right now, it's loud and the crescendo only grows as fire pulses through my veins. "And you'll get full coopera-tion from me on this. Dad messed up by making promises he can't keep, Micah. This is his clusterfuck, but he's not prepared to deal with the fallout."

"What did he do?" Each word leaves me on a barely controlled growl as the hold on my glass tightens. A small crack appeared near the top of the rim by my thumb. "Why is the Armas family being targeted?"

"He pissed off a major campaign donor by not granting him the fast multi-billion dollar purchase and approval to build upon a state park. The area has manmade beaches, but connects to Biscayne Bay and has a lot of eyes on it. He's not the first to want the state-owned land, but the governor hasn't approved—"

"But he trusts your father."

"He'd sign off eventually after getting a cut without a second thought if Dad was backing it."

"So why didn't your Mayor Joaquin Armas agree?"

Lifting his drink, Lionel takes a deep sip, shifting his eyes toward my desk. More importantly toward a sheet of paper I'd somehow missed while his sister was busy distracting me with her treats. "Because Liliana found out and begged him not to. She made him realize he'd be taking away one of the last accessible places in Miami for thousands of families to visit who want to enjoy a peaceful outing while enjoying the beach. Reminded him of all the times they went kayaking—of him teaching me how to fish there."

"And now someone's angry at him."

"Yes, but we never thought anyone would be stupid enough to steal from us. Involve you."

"I want a name, Lionel."

"Rodolfo Diaz." No hesitation. That's all he says, and my world becomes a red haze. If there's one thing I am, it's a man of my word: Liliana Armas is untouchable. *He's a dead man.* The asshole is a developer and works with a large investment group, which my father is a part of. He's also a man who just bit off more than he could chew. "Diaz has been trying to make this happen for a few years now but keeps hitting a wall. No one's giving him the green light, but Dad verbally did before his election."

"I'm guessing he backed out."

"Yeah, he did."

I nod, swirling the contents inside my glass around. In my mind, I'm already seeing the chess game set in front of me and the second of my moves will be made shortly.

The first was when I killed Herbert.

The second comes when I call Alfred back.

This changes things slightly. I'll situate my pieces and unlike the game, I'll kill the fake king.

"You understand I won't take this lightly? That this as a personal insult?"

"I'm as angry as you are."

"Good. Because they're lucky she wasn't home when it happened, or they'd already be dead." And Lionel understands what I mean. On the dates given to me by Alfred, my rebel had been away on a weekend getaway on another one of my ships with her adoptive cousin, Bernice. Three days at sea with port stops at our private island—a playground for those looking to relax, drink, and enjoy the Caribbean waters—and then the Bahamas.

She'd stayed in my private room.

Had security on board and off, following her until she was back home without a single scratch. This was also before her move into her mother's condo.

"I need her to be safe no matter what, Royce. That's all I'm asking for here."

"You have my word. Rebel will always be safe by my side, but are you?"

"I can handle the security for my father and me." Turning a bit, Lionel places a hand on my shoulder and gives it a squeeze. The man before me has a look in his eyes that I'm all too familiar with. This is someone wanting retribution—blood. "I came here knowing something was wrong and with a warning of my own. If something happens, Micah, take care of them. All the information you need is in those papers. Use them however you see fit, but they don't touch Lila or Mom."

"You have my word."

"Thank you, my brother."

AFTER LIONEL LEFT, I stayed inside my office taking care of a phone call from the head of accounting regarding the sudden change in personnel. Not that he could argue with me on it, Andrew Weber was getting a much-needed secretary, but Beverly wasn't exactly what the older male had in mind when it comes to the position.

This man is straight-laced and heavily ruled by propriety. Not one for games.

More so when it comes to making sure every single cent in my company is accounted for and properly disbursed with the proper paper trail to explain the most minute expenditure. I trust him, as did his last assistant who retired a few months ago, and only due to medical reasons.

Since then, the man hasn't been keen on taking anyone new on.

His wife managed their department while he ran the numbers. The husband-and-wife team were seamless for thirty years and I'd hate to see the man go, especially because of this.

Yet there's no one I trust to keep her under rein.

Why I gave him the right to fire her if need be.

"I trust you to make the right decision when it comes to handling Miss Mills, Andrew," I say, my eyes on the information left behind by Lionel. The slim binder held eight pages and the very first was the original proposal with an estimated timeline, budget, and a quick gloss over of the luxury resort Diaz wants the land for. At best, this was a first and very rough draft while the later pages gave detailed information on each member of the investment group, including my father.

Now, the question is why would he try to steal from the son of a partner?

To force compliance if he has something on me.

To ask for more funds in exchange for his possible silence.

It was a very rookie mistake when playing in the water with sharks, and Royce Sr. is no idiot. Neither am I.

"...I'll do what I can, Mr. Royce. She's already made quite the impression today with the two junior accountants on my team." Andrew takes a pause; on the other end of the call, I can make out the squeaking of a chair and then the closing of a door. "They'd asked for copies of last month's performer payroll from the Diamante line. We wanted to cross reference hours clocked from the last six months, but she refused. Simply told them it wasn't part of her job."

"Her job is what you say it is." Movement on my computer screen catches my eyes and I look up, catching a still-here Liliana walk to her desk. It's normal for the cameras in her office to always run in the background, to highlight her office, but right now it doesn't bring me the joy it usually does. Not when I catch sight of what she has in her hands. *The fuck.* "Not up for discussion. Another strike, and I expect you to fire her."

"Of course, sir."

"It's Micah to you, old man. You've been with us for a very long time." At my response, his laughter filters through but then fades into nothing. I see a roll of tape in her hands and some cardboard. I watch her move, rise onto the tips of her toes to remove a few picture frames, and I'm standing before she's done. "Do what you must and report back. I trust you, Andrew."

"Thank you, Micah. I'll be in touch."

"We'll talk soon."

I end the call before the last syllable passes through my lips. In the background, it sounds like he said something else, but I pay no heed. I'm across the room in seconds and out the door, marching toward her office without stopping and entering the space just the same.

At once our eyes meet, those beautiful hazel orbs widening with shock while her lips part and a teasing touch of pink sweeps across her cheeks. As if she's been caught doing something inappropriate.

And in that moment, I give no fucks about propriety. I don't care about anything but stopping her.

"Where the hell are you going, Rebel?"

Chapter 6
LILIANA

"Where the hell are you going, Rebel?"

"Shouldn't it be obvious, Mr. Royce?" Without looking up, I continue putting together a cardboard box—my movements hold a bit of sulking—to help me shift my belongings downstairs like the other assistants. I'm not angry at Micah, but I'm losing my constant access to him. To his scent. *Being away from you is going to be torture.* "I did accept your offer."

"Put the box down, Liliana," Micah grits out, and I shift my gaze just so I can show him I'm rolling my eyes. What I find, though, causes my heart to race for a different reason: he's angry. He's also a lot closer than I thought. On the other side of my desk and glaring, his lip curls over his teeth in disgust while those hypnotizing blue eyes switch between the box in my hand and the mess atop my desk. *Even upset, he's a god among men.* "Don't be a brat, and do as I say."

"Can't." My shrug only serves to further upset him, and I'm given a taste of his frosty gaze a second later. Which doesn't make sense since he's the one changing my position. He's the one that made the rule about his assistants working a floor below him. "I've got too much to do, and wasting time isn't in the script today. Please let me get back to it."

"I sent you home."

"And I need to get this done."

His nostrils flare at my response while he holds out his open palm. "Hand it over and go home."

"No." Sass with a touch of annoyance, and he's not impressed. Instead, I'm growled at while he prowls around to my side, stopping only when his towering frame disrupts my personal space. The fabric of his suit skims my side, causing a small ripple of pleasure to rock me where I stand. "W-What are you doing?"

"Give. It."

"Micah, this isn't making any sense. Assistants belong one floor down—"

"So help me God, Liliana," he snarls, and for the first time in all the years I've known him, I experience his vexation. Moreover, it's directed at me, and I don't like it. "Don't test me. Give me the box and go home. That's an order."

"You're the one being difficult." And confusing. And so fucking handsome it causes every muscle in my body to contract with need. Even like this, angry at me for reasons that evade rationality, I can't help but respond to him. The shiver that coasts up my spine. The wetness coating my inner thighs now. "Doesn't this new position mean I'm moving a floor—"

"No."

"No, what?"

"No. You're not going anywhere." Each word is spat out through clenched teeth. "And I suggest you get rid of that thing before I do it for you."

"Are you serious right now? How am I supposed to...hey!"

"Warned you." That's all he says before the box is ripped from my hold and then broken into three uneven pieces. Micah tosses the remnants aside, knocking a gold-leafed frame with a picture of the night he stole my first kiss to the ground.

In it, I'm standing with Lionel to my right while he occupies my left, each smirking into the lens while I'm blushing profusely. To this day, I blame it on spending the day out on the beach, hanging with friends, and then the game of volleyball my brother started and I won.

Not because he showed up late and then gave me the best gift.

Not because he'd given my heart hope, short-lived as it was.

"You kept our secret," he says, pulling me out of my thoughts and bringing me into focus. Micah's squatting a few feet from me and smiling, the still pristine frame in his hand. The glass didn't crack and there are no scratches, but what has me transfixed is the smile on his lips. How he looks at the frozen moment in time my mother captured and then placed on my office shelves the day I took my original position as part of his IT department.

She was so proud of me that day. Of her daughter following her dreams while putting to use the set of skills developed during my early teens. Because when nothing else made sense—he didn't return my feelings—coding never failed me.

It did what I wanted it to. Our relationship wasn't one-sided or muddled by titles and who I'm related to. My input was received and always gave the desired outcome, not caring who my big brother was.

Programs are predictable. Sequences that make up strings are dependable.

But it never quite filled the void in my heart.

"I did."

"One day soon, I'm going to reward you for that."

"What does that mean, Micah?" Because he's never brought that night up. Never gave me an inkling that it meant anything. "You're confusing me."

Standing to his full height, he towers over me while the warmth coming off his body wraps around me. We're so close. His scent makes me feel a little drunk on him, but it's the touch of his fingers tipping my chin that weakens my knees. I sway a bit where I stand, feeling the warmth where we connect, but his hold on my face remains firm.

Strong yet gentle fingers keep my eyes on Micah while he gifts me my smile. A little crooked and sinful, but mine. "It means I have years' worth of things to make up for. And I'm a man who pays his debts, sweet Rebel. I plan to spoil you."

I'VE BEEN THINKING about our interaction—his words—since coming back to my mother's condo.

It's been a few hours since he walked out of my office after removing every available box I'd dragged in from storage to help me move my workspace down a floor. He wasn't happy with my assumption that I'd be leaving. Micah's heated look bore into the side of my face as I tried my best to ignore him while putting things back in their place.

That put him at ease. Removed the heaviness in the room as he waited for me to be done.

Then, and only then, did he walk out, but not before dragging me with him. I was walked to my car, buckled in, and told to go home and that he'd let everyone in the lobby know not to let me in until after midday tomorrow.

Not my usual start time of nine, but twelve o'clock and not a second sooner because of my disobedience.

"That's your punishment, Rebel. Undermine me again, and I'll

make sure it stings. "

That's how he sent me off, not realizing just how much those words affected me.

My body and mind were in sync when it came to him, and I wanted to test his warning. To see just how he'd make it *sting*.

Because I might be a virgin, but that doesn't change my biological need for this man. Lust and love dominate me, two sides of the coin, yet they come together to torture my every waking moment.

I wish for the day he bends me over any available surface and takes me.

I pray every night for him to love me. See me.

"Maybe working with him isn't such a good—" I'm cut off by the sudden ringing of my doorbell and look up. It chimes throughout the house, forcing me to pad out of my room after dropping the cozy camisole and shorts set I pulled out of my still-unpacked luggage and was seconds from slipping into. Cooking tonight was going to be a simple affair, as were my plans of spending the night under my covers while watching a movie.

Maybe with a glass of wine. A little chocolate for dessert.

Rushing to the door, I peek out through the keyhole and find no one in the hallway. Completely empty.

"Weird." I'm not worried about my safety. This building is owned by a friend of my father, one of his donor/golf buddies, and the security downstairs is tight. No one is let up without being approved or signed in, so I open the door and immediately my attention is brought down to the ground. Set up on a pedestal-like contraption is takeout from one of my favorite eateries, and I squeal.

This beats my plans of mac and cheese and the half a bottle of a Chilean wine I have in the fridge. It's a fruity red with notes of spice that pair well with the richness of my favorite comfort dish, but will now be exceptional with the brick-oven pizza and what I'm sure is one of each signature desserts the restaurant offers.

My mouth waters as the aroma permeates the hall and I find

myself smiling as I pick everything up. Once again, Micah's words from earlier today, a different conversation, rush through my head:

Expect a treat from me tonight. It'll be there at six.

And it's confirmed after I set everything down on my kitchen counter, finding a note attached to the lip of the bag. I recognize his writing while a quick flick of my eyes toward the wall clock gives me the time.

The man is punctual.

He's also killing me.

I'm a man of my word and pay all of my debts. I promised to spoil you, my little Rebel.

Your Boss,
Mr. Royce

"Why are you doing this to me?" Doesn't he realize how much a gesture like this builds giddy excitement within me? How I've created castles in the sky in his honor, and each sweet gesture only erects another tower in his name? "Micah Royce will always be my ruin."

Yet as the words leave me, I'm already opening the box and a few seconds later, giggling. He knows I love a good Margherita pizza, the combination of mozzarella and basil is heaven to me, but to literally have them spell out the words *stuck with me* in basil makes my night.

Because even after everything and knowing my feelings are one-sided, I can't help but melt at the adorableness of this gift. Sure, his meaning and mine are vastly different—one day I'll move away and find someone to love and adore me back—but for now, this soothes me.

Lets me live in a make-believe world where he's a man taking care of his woman. Where I'm wanted by him, and my every need is met while I return every gesture with one of my own.

It's why I will stay as his assistant for now.

It's why I grab a plate with two slices and my wine before heading to the couch, bypassing the few boxes I've yet to open. Nothing of mine has been unpacked and this gives out *living out of my suitcase* vibes, but that's okay. Instead of worrying over my lack of desire to make this place homey, I return to my original plan of finding a movie or a show between bites.

And while I still turn on my TV and put on a random house-flipping show for background noise…

I'm enticed by something else.

A calling. This itch.

At the edge of my coffee table lies a black and gold notebook that I don't hesitate to pick up. There's a pen clipped on the page with my last entry, and I read the quick lines jotted down in a messy scrawl that indicates I was in a hurry. The feelings are the same; my love for him is clear and honest, but what surprises me is the coincidence in topic.

This goes back to him asking me to keep another secret. Not so much for him, but in case anyone asked how much I make at Royce Cruise Line—especially from those in my department. And while I found it odd then, I nodded but came back to the same torturous memory:

My first kiss.

The feel of him against me.

Diosito, I need help here. Help me find a fault in him.

Maybe if I knocked him off the pedestal I placed him on, I'd be able to move on.

Yet none of those things happen. Instead, I simply finish my delicious pizza and then grab two mini cannoli before settling back. One show has ended and another one begins to play, the same renovation type that usually draws me in, but I'm still pulled in by that last entry.

It doesn't take long for me to click the pen and place it against a new sheet of paper.

It's seconds before the words tumble out of me and emotions fill each line…

A single taste of you will never be enough.
You stole my heart.

Chapter 7
LILIANA

EIGHTEEN CANDLES...

"**H**appy birthday to you. Happy Birthday to you…" a voice croons near my ear and I jump, whirling around to face the culprit. Because I'd know that voice anywhere, missed him today, and yet nothing matters more than enjoying him this close. His scent envelops me, and it takes every ounce of my almost nonexistent self-control not to lean in closer. To not nuzzle my face against his chest and drown in the moment. "Happy eighteenth birthday, you pretty little rebel."

"You're never going to let that go, are you?" I groan as a small smile tugs at my lips. It's also a deflection; I'd rather let him think I'm embarrassed than let him know the truth…

That he affects me. That my heart beats for him.

"Not a chance in hell." Lifting a hand, he brings it toward my dark hair and gives the beachy waves a tug. He doesn't let go of the strand after like he'd typically do. Instead, Micah wraps it around a long digit while exhaling roughly. "It's one of my fondest memories."

A step closer. He's invading my personal space.

"Where have you been? And are you serious?" All day, I've been searching for him—hoping to be gifted one of his warm hugs—but for the first time since we met, Micah let me down. A part of me is a little disappointed he wasn't here to cut my cake or join the party, but I still smile at him and it's genuine.

He's nodding before I'm done with my questions. "Meetings with the old man and a few vendors. And two, that day you cemented your legacy at our high school for being an anarchist." Amusement comes through his tone, but there's also something that feels a lot like pride. Like he loved the little rebellion I accidentally caused the entire student body to join. I was mad at the faculty for the unjust ten-day suspension of a friend of mine for simply defending herself from a man who made her uncomfortable.

She told him to fuck off amongst other colorful things, and the staff member who heard her never thought to get the whole story. Not because this office employee was a bad person, but because they didn't think past what they saw as disrespect toward an adult who was simply there to make a scheduled delivery to the cafeteria at our expensive institution.

My friend wasn't being a brat. She wasn't looking down at this man because of a tax bracket.

No, she was a sixteen-year-old girl who didn't like the way he looked or spoke to her and told him just that in a very colorful way. And I made sure the entire school knew how I felt, which created an avalanche. One person told another, and soon we were all out of class and protesting.

I might have hacked the office computers too.

I might have made it so they couldn't do anything but look at the screen replaying a donkey's ass for two days.

"But Nessa was back the next day with a full apology, and the man was reported to his company."

"She was." His beautiful blue eyes soften. "You did so good."

"Thank you." Heat sweeps across my skin, but this time it's because he's released my hair and is now tracing the same finger down my arm. Goosebumps rise and a shiver runs down my spine, one I can't disguise as anything but what it is: his effect on me. "Too bad you guys had graduated by then...wait. How did you find out so quickly?"

One minute I was chanting with the crowd, and the next I had a human shield on each side. Lionel and Micah had appeared out of nowhere and the principal, who had been shouting threats and demanding we return to class or else, backed off.

No repercussions. The entire staff at the school was mandated to attend special training.

"We were in the area."

"That makes no—" I'm cut off by the sudden feel of his lips. Perfectly warm and soft, Micah slants his mouth over mine, taking from me what I give so easily. What I've saved for him; all my firsts are his if he wants them. Every bit of me, and I've never been happier with a decision I've made.

This was a corruptively earth-shattering moment; I'm left weak-kneed and grabbing onto the front of his white shirt, using him to remain upright. Not that I have to worry as a second later, his strong arm wraps around my back and tugs me closer. One yank and we're pressed together without any space between us, and I moan at the feel of his chest pressing against mine.

Which makes no sense with our size difference, but then I notice my feet are no longer touching the sand. Micah's picked me up, one thick arm supporting my weight, and I've never felt more delicate. More his, and I whimper when his teeth rake down my bottom lip, an action that pulls another moan from me, and he takes advantage of that.

I feel his possessive hunger as he slips his tongue over mine, *caressing, while his other hand cups the back of my neck. He angles my head and deepens the kiss, devours me, before exploring every inch of my mouth. His groans vibrate through me, a sound that makes my thighs clench in his hold. That makes me chase his lips and suck a little on the tip of his tongue.*

An action he approves of. His following growl and the prominent bulge in his pants are proof of that.

And every one of my processors is on overload, creating a delicious havoc within that in a way settles me. Hard and soft, opposite ends of the spectrum, and yet they complement each other. That's how this feels.

It's right.

It's meant to be.

Micah slows down the kiss to a few slow pecks. "Fuck, *Rebel. You're so sweet.*"

"*Please.*" *It's all I manage to whimper. I need more. All of him.*

In the distance, I hear laughter and it's coming in the direction of the beach party turned late-night club. The pool area and ballroom of a luxurious hotel were rented out by my parents for the occasion, giving my friends and family plenty of time to play and let loose. Their clapping and the loud music mean only one thing: they're dancing.

More than likely in a rueda; a style of salsa dancing that originated in my parents' home country. Here, the couples form a large circle where the steps, turns, and patterns are executed in unison—choreographed—to the calls of the singer or the group's leader.

And for a few seconds after, the hold on the back of my neck and hip tightens, as does the feel of his mouth on mine. He breathes in my every exhale. His teeth embed themselves into my bottom lip and those gorgeous blue eyes I adore close.

My heart races while he swallows hard.

My pussy clenches while I feel him throb against me.

I did that to him. He's finally—

"*Jesus, Liliana.*"

"Micah, I—"

He lays his forehead against mine and exhales roughly. "Happy Birthday, sweetheart. That's all I wanted to say to you before..." under his breath he mutters a low *fuck* then schools his features *"...this needs to stay our little secret. Just ours, Liliana. Can you do that for me?"*

"Yes." I lick my lips, and his eyes follow the movement. The intent is there to kiss me again, but then I'm placed on my feet and he takes a step back. Then another. Micah makes sure to put a respectable amount of distance between us and a few seconds later, I understand why.

My brother approaches us, his smile wide. "Dude, you finally got here!"

"Yeah. My meetings ran late, and I stopped to give the birthday girl my gift."

Did he plan this? Why ask me to keep it a secret?

"...did you eat? There's plenty of food inside, and Mom saved you your favorite." If my brother notices the lack of a gift box or card, he doesn't call his best friend out on it. Instead, he slips between us and throws an arm around Micah's shoulder and then mine, pulling us together in a sideways hug. He is slick in the way he turns us toward the party and away from the near-black water's edge, but I catch on and meet Micah's eyes again.

They're heated, but then clear. "I did. I'm more than satisfied."

"Okay. I'm sure we can find a take-home container for the Cuban tamales." As he says this, my brother pulls ahead, releasing us both. The distance isn't big, but enough that Micah sends me a wink and mouths the words: pretty little secret.

I awake with a start, my body thrumming the same way it did that night. I'm shaking and my chest rises and falls rapidly; I can almost feel his kiss even after all these years. I'm also not sure of how I got into bed last night, not after polishing off the rest of the bottle and pouring my emotions onto page after page in my journal.

It felt good. A reflective moment, but even today I can still smell him around me.

It's faint. The taste of a memory.

He's crisp citrus with notes of smooth bourbon, sensual and warm, and I constantly crave him. And while I usually stick to my red wines, I won't deny that I have an opened bottle of Kentucky Owl for those nights when I need a reprieve.

A few sips of that, and then my Womanizer helps take the edge off.

Is that what happened last night? Did I switch to bourbon and that's why I don't remember crawling into bed? *But then why don't I feel hungover?*

"I'm so fucked." In many ways, and yet, I'm already skimming a hand down between my thighs, and I'm not surprised to find my underwear soaked. The gusset clings to my mound, molding over my clit and labia before digging a little into my clenching hole. It's searching for him; my body craves his touch—to be owned for the first time.

At almost twenty-three, I'm ready for more.

To not wake up alone anymore. To fall to my knees or spread them wide.

Slipping my fingers beneath the waistband, I tremble at the first feather-like touch over my clit. It's swollen and slick with my arousal, the sensation causing me to whimper as my hips buck. I'm needy and the faintest touch has my eyes closing, and it's his face I see behind my lids.

His plump lips as I form a V with two fingers and spread my lips, rubbing across each one before slightly dipping the tips into my entrance. Just a tease, but God does it feel good. More so when I imagine his heated eyes looking at me just the way he did the night we kissed.

"*Micah.*" Another moan, my hips following my fingers, pushing me closer to a release that will never fully fulfill me. Yet I chase it. Need it. "Please, Papi."

A warm rush of wetness coats my hand and I shiver, but it's when I rub two tight circles over my clit that pleasure rocks me. I'm so sensitive, swollen, and I come while doing nothing more than holding those slick fingers against my bundle of nerves.

Light pressure. No movement.

And fuck me if I don't scream out his name like the prayer that it is. Pleasure rocks me and I'm shaking, riding each wave until the last one leaves me and I'm drifting off once more.

God, I needed that.

But more than that, I'm desperate for him.

THE PINGING of my phone pulls me from sleep, and this time when I open my eyes the sun is high in the sky. It streams in from my sheer curtains, bathing the room in more light than I'm used to first thing in the morning.

Next, I'm aware of the vibrating of my phone. That first alert wasn't a call or alarm. No, it's the reminder that a text came in and I haven't responded.

Stretching my arms up, I turn just enough to reach the device and angle it so it picks up my face, unlocking the screen. It does in seconds and leads me right to that message, my heart giving a gentle tug when I see it's from Micah.

> You're late, Miss Armas. ~Captain Grumps

Immediately my eyes flick to the time in the upper left of my screen, and I shoot out of bed. "How the hell?"

Not that I've never done this on the weekends—sleeping is my third greatest love after coffee and Micah—but workdays are sacred. I'm always on time. No excuses.

It's one in the afternoon, and I quickly throw my legs over the edge of the bed, dragging the comforter with me. Second on the agenda is calling him, and I do, only having to wait for two rings before it connects.

For a beat or two, silence filters through right before he chuckles.

"You're such a bad girl, Rebel. Didn't think I'd need to reprimand you so soon."

His words...

That edge with a hint of playfulness...

It makes me shiver while my core clenches, my pulse racing as what I did a few hours ago to calm my need is rendered useless. I'm right back to yesterday and the memory of that kiss, fighting my body and the whimper trying to break free but I have no choice but to swallow it back.

I have seconds to respond, to make up an excuse, and when I do, what slips out surprises us both. I've never done this since starting at his company.

"I'm actually calling you to take the day off, Mr. Royce."

Chapter 8
LILIANA

"There's my baby girl," Mom squeals three days later, rushing over and crushing me in a warm hug. She's been gone a while now, but then again, that's been her modus operandi since divorcing Dad. Vacations and self-discovery trips mixed with reliving her youth, or anything she feels she missed by becoming Joaquin Armas's wife. "How have you been?"

"I'm good, and happy you're home." It's the truth. We all miss her. "But other than that, busy with work."

It's not a lie. Since coming back after taking a self-care day to readjust my armor, I've been left alone to deal with "extras" outside of his daily itinerary. He's been away from headquarters while I've sat down with two department heads and gone over reports that are above my pay grade. Sure, I understand numbers, and what they presented are documents I'm used to logging for him as his *under-cover* secretary, but this was more.

This showed trust. Micah would never allow Beverly to handle any of his meetings.

I miss him, though.

"Miss Armas, here are the talent payroll reports I promised Mr. Royce. He asked me to give them to you, and if you have a minute, I'd like to explain a few things." Startled by the man's voice, I nearly drop my bottle of water and in the midst of catching it, my ear bud pops loose. That would've been helpful a minute ago as I would've heard his approach, or better yet, the elevator, but I wasn't expecting anyone today. Micah's been out at the Royce shipyard since the day after he all but forbid me from occupying the secretary's desk a floor below us.

He's overseeing the installation of the new top deck pool area for Esmeralda. She's his baby at the moment, a complete redesign of the style his family's cruise line is known for, and while I'm dying to have him back at the office, I'm proud of him. Excited to see the final product after getting a glimpse from a folder on his desk.

"You scared me, Mr. Weber. Of course. Please follow me to my office," I say, gripping both items while waving my empty hand toward my door.

"My apologies, Miss—"

"It's Liliana, please."

"Of course, Liliana. Lead the way." A huff comes from behind him and I take a quick look, finding a petulant Beverly. She's holding a file and iPad, but before I can address her, Mr. Weber is giving her a look I've never seen the older man give anyone. "Do you have a problem, Miss Mills?"

"No, sir." It's grit out.

He doesn't say anything else to her, but I catch the glare before he turns and gives me a smile. It's warm and kind of reminds me of the ones my abuelo gave me before passing away. "Please lead the way, Liliana."

Giving them a nod, I lead them away from the kitchenette and toward my domain. My computers are running at the moment. I'm giving our system an extra malware scan to make sure nothing has been tampered with since our last scheduled testing. Big companies like these are always at risk; the most minute oversight could cost the Royces millions, and that's something I won't allow.

Am I doing this outside of my department's knowledge? Yes.

Do I trust everyone in this company? No.

Something isn't right, and after the attempted robbery in Micah's stateroom, I'm keeping a tighter watch on things. I don't care what the head of the IT department thinks.

Once inside my office, they take a seat across from me. Mr. Weber is polite and asks for permission to spread his report across my desk, and while I nod, I take note of how Beverly stares at the large monitor behind me. It's a new addition, brought in and installed by me without permission to run multiple channels at once. That one is going through the backup server now, a private program I've been using in conjunction with ours.

"What do you think you're doing?"

"Look at this line, Liliana." They speak in unison with the latter sending her another disgruntled glower, but I don't pay her question any attention. Her saltiness isn't a concern for me. I'll keep an eye on her, though. *That tone and the sudden flash of anger are about more than just losing her position. "There's been an elevation in unauthorized overtime that I want Mr. Royce to be made aware of."*

"Of course, Mr. Webber. Show me, and I'll make sure he becomes aware of the situation."

"And how is Captain Grumps these days?" Mom raises her brow at that while I prepare myself for what's coming. She's the only one outside of my cousin Bernice that knows of my feelings for Micah, from my crush to my love and every moment in between, except for our one and only kiss. And while she isn't around as much now, something I don't begrudge her, we still catch up once a week, and he's always a large chunk of that conversation.

"*Captain Grumps* is fine. Being a little dictator here and there, but fine." Just like his nickname for me has stuck over the years, mine for him has too. At least for me and Mom and Bernice. She gets a kick out of using the code word—never in front of him—while I let her have her fun.

"By the way, I heard you got a promotion."

At that, I raise a brow, my lips pursing. "How do *you* know that?"

Mom shrugs while taking a quick peek at her smartwatch before meeting my eyes again. "There's been some talk."

"Talk? About?"

"Your father wants your help with some pre-campaign ground-work, but Lionel told him no." That surprises me. My brother isn't one to go against our father, not unless there's a good reason. "He called me to join forces, too."

"And why is everyone discussing this without consulting me?" As soon as I finish my question, the conveyor belt begins to move. Luggage from her flight starts coming through, tumbling down, and I recognize her hard-shell floral ones immediately, gripping them and yanking the two off. They're both all-wheel spinners and with ease I turn them, maneuvering us through the claim area and down the elevator to the level that connects with parking.

"Holy moly." She exclaims the second we walk outside, fanning herself while ignoring my question. I get it, though. The heat this year has been brutal thus far. "Que calor, Mamita."

"I know. And they say it's only going to get worse."

"Hopefully we stay hurricane free this year."

"Cross your fingers." I'm parked near the entrance, and it takes mere minutes to get in and complain about how hot the all-black leather seats are before heading out and taking the exit out of Miami International. We're heading toward my father's real house, not the mayoral mansion he occupies during the week as part of the illusion and position.

Wonder why he asked to have dinner at home, though?

"Lili, we didn't mention anything because we'd rather save you the frustration and then the argument that'll follow. To be honest, baby, that man is so clueless sometimes. Your dad's not a bad man, loves you guys dearly, but his tunnel vision is his biggest downfall." There's a hint of annoyance in her tone, and it's not weather-related. From the corner of my eyes, I look over and catch her shaking her head. Mom's expression is a bit complicated, wistful yet longing. "He forgets that this family is now full of adults with their own lives and we're no longer his staff."

"That's mean, Mom."

"It's the truth, Liliana." An exasperated huff tinged with bitterness follows. "Joaquin Armas had the audacity to get upset because I reminded him of that. Of the fact you're graduating soon and don't have time to run his political image."

"I am good at it, though."

"Do you really want to—"

"Heck no," I say, then snort. "Dad's the biggest micro-manager I've ever met."

"Then why are you defending him?"

"Because someone has to," I say, voice neutral. I'm not looking to argue with her. Something she tries to do a second later. Her lips part and I can almost see the retort coming, but I hold a hand up while slightly merging onto the highway. "He has flaws, Mom. I know that, but so do you. No one in our family isn't without some kind of idiosyncrasy that makes the rest of us want to pull our hair out."

———

"Look who finally decided to grace us with her presence."

"Why are we here again? You never come here during the week." A bit snide. Huffy.

Dad merely shrugs, lips quirking up in a smirk. "Because this is *our* home."

"Shut it, Joaquin." Mom steps fully into the family room and heads straight for the man she's scowling at. They watch each other for a second before hugging, his arms wrapping around her while whispering something in her ear. Her annoyance with him lasts as long as mine with Micah—you can't help who you love.

That's also about the time I walk out of the room, giving them a few moments to talk while heading toward the kitchen. There's a lot of noise coming from in there, what sound like pots and pans and then a squeal, the latter coming from Bernice who's pulling her soaked shirt away from her body.

Lionel is on the opposite side of the island, smirking at her while holding the detachable faucet in his hand. "Take it back."

"You are such a child!"

"Says the one yelling like one?"

"Is this what you two do when I'm not around?" I say and give one solid clap, causing their heads to simultaneously snap in my direction, each with a different expression. One is smug while the other goes timid, and it's *her* I focus on. Bernice isn't our cousin by blood, but because I adopted her into our clan.

Not literally, but of the heart.

I met her in school a year after we met Micah, and we just clicked. Our group in school was tiny; I can count on one hand the girlfriends I trusted over the years—those who stuck around—but she's always been the closest to me. The one who got in trouble with me.

The one who came up with the crazy plans that got us in trouble in the first place.

Everyone's accepted her because of me, but there's always been a teasing edge between my brother and her. Right now, she's blushing and clenching the hand not pulling the fabric away from her body.

There's also the subtle way they keep sneaking glances, or more like glaring at each other.

Will they ever give in?

"Well?" Arching a brow, I cock my hip to the side. "Who's going to explain this mess?"

"I will." My body stiffens, goosebumps rising across my skin as *his* warm breath skims the back of my neck a second before a tint trickle of cold water runs down the back of my shirt...

Chapter 9
MICAH

EARLIER THAT DAY...

"I want answers, Alfred." We're standing beneath Esmeralda, the crane to the left of us done for the day, but I'd ordered the driver to leave the long chain and anchor attached dangling a few feet above Alfred's head. It's not going to fall, but I do get a kick out of watching him squirm.

Looking up every few minutes. Sweating. Trying to shift, but a single arch of my brow makes him stop.

Pussy.

"Sir, I—"

"You have ten seconds to give me a name. Lie to me, and you'll make it home in a body bag."

"It's not as easy. They'll come after my family—"

"Five, four…" I hold a hand out, and Isaac places a Glock in it "…three, two—"

"Rodolfo Diaz."

"See? That wasn't so hard." My finger on the trigger twitches and the gun goes off, the bullet grazing Alfred's thigh. A flesh wound to match the others I've already given him, but the way he screams, you'd think I amputated his leg. "Take that as my last warning, Mr. Castillo. Don't test my patience."

"Yes, sir." A whimper. He's shaking while a piss stain forms on the front of his jeans.

"Now, what do we know about Rodolfo's whereabouts?"

"Mr. Diaz didn't act alone." That piques my interest, and I wave the hand with the gun for him to continue. Swallowing hard, Alfred stumbles a bit as he presses a hand on the wound—it's bleeding, but not enough for the theatrics. "Can I please sit?"

The next shot marks where I'll allow him to drop. It's by his feet and the concrete shatters, shards splintering around him. "Get on the ground."

"Thank you." He struggles, shaking, but eventually sits. "I'm not trying to be difficult, Mr. Royce. Just want to protect my children."

"I won't ask again, Alfred. Last chance." Lifting the gun so the aim is at his head, I smile. "What do you know?"

"His son is involved."

"Hmmm." Not surprising in the least. Brian Diaz has been after his father's approval for years and has yet to do more than be his lackey. One never dirties his hands while the other makes deals and promises larger the family bank accounts, but this one crossed the line. I'd never given a shit about them or anyone Royce Sr. has done business with in the past, but this time it's personal. "That isn't enough, and you know it. Don't make me hurt you again."

Subconsciously, Alfred touches the scars on his face; they're red and angry. The jagged lines on his cheek look a little infected and he flinches, shaking the same way he did the night I gifted him this token of appreciation. No one tries to steal from me or mine and walks away empty handed.

Swallowing hard, Alfred looks down at my shoes. Focuses on them. "It goes beyond a working relationship, though, Mr. Royce. I got my hands on the emails between him and Herbert. They're in my car."

"How beyond?"

"Intimately."

"Then you should've led with that." Looking back at my guards, I nod at the one standing just behind Isaac. "Ligo, take him to retrieve whatever files he has and bring back my mother-in-law's safe. I do imagine you were smart enough to bring it with you, Alfred?"

"Yes, sir."

"Good. Make it quick." Struggling, Alfred gets up and walks away with my security while Isaac steps up beside me, facing the water. For a few moments we don't talk, but I can sense there's something on his mind. "Speak up."

"Do you trust this asshole?"

"Not in the least." My eyes are fixed on the horizon as I tuck the gun into the back of my pants. Miami is a beautiful city, but the water calls to me. There's a sense of sereneness—pull—to the ocean that's deceptive. What's calm can turn turbulent in the blink of an eye. From innocent prey to vicious hunters, the sea is a map of traps with plenty of warnings, and it all depends on whose area you play in to know how fatal the bite will be.

I understand that. Respect it. Yet like the darkest blue, a true monster hides within me, and he's close to the surface right now. Angry. Full of the need to spill blood.

The Diaz men have made a grave mistake. One I will take more than my pound of flesh for.

"Then why not—"

"Because I'm not leaving his children fatherless." I may not have plans to kill Alfred Castillo at the moment, but he will atone for his sins. Moreover, I've done my research on the man, have people watching his family, and he is a doting father. Dumb as shit, but good to them, and I'll make sure he never puts anyone he loves in danger again. It's what my rebel would want me to do. "But if he steps a single foot out of line…"

"Understood, boss. We'll treat him right."

"Good." From behind us, I hear the scuffing of shoes on the pavement and the whimpers of pain coming from the informant. They're close, but before they reach us, I turn and look at Isaac. "I want Ligo moved to Liliana's protection effective immediately. Two more will work under him, but make sure he's aware that if a single hair on her head is harmed, I'll personally strap him to the bottom of one of my ships and drag his corpse through the Caribbean while letting predators feed on his remains as we travel from port to port."

———

"You're a dead man, Royce," she growls, and I swear it's like a kitten's grumbly purr. Soft and sweet with just the right touch of *pet me please* in her tone, Liliana whirls around to face me. Her eyes flash with ire and her lips part with a sharp retort sitting on that pink tongue, but then her entire being simmers into a different kind of heat as she gets a good look at what I'm wearing:

A pair of dark denim jeans with a rip on the left knee.

A black T-shirt that strains across my chest.

An old pair of Chuck Taylors I've never thrown away.

Is it playing dirty that I'd been wearing this the night I stole her first kiss? Yes, but I'm not an honorable man when it comes to her. For her, I'll do whatever it takes to always be the center of her world, as she is mine.

Those charming hazel eyes peruse my body from head to sneakers and back up again, pausing over my tattooed sleeve before unconsciously biting her bottom lip. They travel over every line and shadow there, a piece she's very familiar with, but it's almost as if she's seeing it for the first time all over again. The nautical-themed artwork—from the thick ropes wrapped around my wrist to the tentacles of an octopus ripping through the water and toward an imposing ship with the name *Royce* in Old English font near the front. There's also a great white shark, her favorite marine animal, on the top of my right hand swimming just beneath what looks to be calmer waters, a complete contrast to the rest of the tattoo.

She appreciates my six-foot-four frame, taking me fully in, and goosebumps rise on my skin. It feels like a caress—my cock begins to swell and throb for her—but before I can say anything, her parents walk into the room.

They pause and stare at us, and it's almost like being in high school all over again. For a brief moment, I recall something...

This happened in our teen years. Almost the same exact scenario, and I smirk down at the now-blushing woman who stands a few inches from me. Back then, we'd been shitheads with vendettas against the girls who'd attacked us with silly string right after winning a college baseball game—in front of everyone our freshmen year—and we'd gotten revenge via an avalanche of over a hundred water balloons a week later.

They'd gotten us at our new school, and we attacked at theirs.

I was a teenager then and knew pranking her back was all I could do at the moment, but now...*fuck*. The man currently standing in her father's kitchen only wants to get her wet one way. Nothing else will suffice. Her place is sitting on my face or clenching around my cock.

She's the only person in this world I'd gladly drop to my knees for.

Back then, though, both our parents wore the same look Mrs. Armas has right now: pure, unadulterated amusement. A bit of incredulity.

"You four are too old for this," Joaquin says, eyes pinging between each of us before shaking his head. It's not from disappointment. The man isn't the easiest person to deal with—his dry nature can be hard to swallow at times—but he loves his family, and that saves him from my response. My respect for him solely lies in my rebel's happiness. "But it's nice to have everyone at home."

"Good to see you too, Dad." Liliana walks past me, giving me a small elbow to the ribs before rising onto the tips of her toes and giving him a quick kiss on the cheek. "Bendicion."

"Que Dios te bendiga." His expression softens immediately before giving her a quick hug and then turning his face toward his ex-wife. "See. This is love."

"Am I supposed to ask you for your blessings every time I see you, dear?" It's snooty, but teasing. She's being coquettish with him, and he's eating it up. *Idiot.* I'd never let Liliana leave me, nor would I give her a reason to want to. "Would that make you happy?"

"It's a step in the right direction."

"Keep dreaming."

"I will—"

"Why don't we all head toward the dining room while the girls get changed," Lionel interrupts, his lips twitching at their flirting. Although separated legally, they're closer now than when they were married.

"That's a great idea, son." Blowing him a quick kiss, she immediately turns toward her ex and huffs. "You heard him."

"Woman, I swear." Joaquin narrows his eyes at Celia, yet he complies and she winks at us before they exit the room. No one says anything for a minute or two, but then Liliana cracks up, which causes Bernice to follow, both girls slapping the nearest thing to them—

Bernice the counter. Rebel my arm.

"And they say we need to grow up?" Lionel grumbles, shooting me a quick look I understand. Behind the laughter and playing around, there's a sobering moment that tells me he has news on Diaz. My nod is barely perceptible but understood. We'll talk before the night is through, but right now, I toss the bottle of water in my hand at him and take hold of the tiny fingers currently digging into my other forearm—which I give a tiny tug to—and a giggling Liliana follows.

I lead her out of the kitchen and down an unlit hallway toward the back of the house that I'm very familiar with. This was her sacred space until she moved out, and even now, I know nothing's changed on the other side of the door we're currently standing in front of. Just like it hasn't for Lionel, who splits his time between this house and an apartment close to their downtown office.

"Change, Rebel. You're cold."

"I'm not—"

I stop her protest with a single finger over her plump lips while my other hand wraps around her waist, tugging her closer. "You. Are." We're almost chest to abdomen, and I make sure my voice is low as I bend my head just low enough that my lips are next to her ear. "Don't lie."

"I'm not...damnit, Micah!" My fingers are now splayed and pressing the back of her wet shirt firmly against her skin. She shivers, and I smirk. "Fine. Now leave."

"Good girl, and no."

"No?" She ignores my praise but tilts her head to the side. Blushing a little, too. "Why?"

"Because I'm not walking into that dining room without you."

THIS ISN'T my first dinner at the Armas home and I groan, sitting back while taking a deep pull from my beer bottle: a crisp Cuban lager with mildly sweet notes. It's always been a popular stock item in their fridge, and even my family has been known to order a couple of cases at a time from the "hook up" Joaquin has on the island.

As mayor, he moves inconspicuously through the city, and more so through the large and not always monitored ports.

"So what's next on the agenda, Mom?" Liliana asks, forking her final piece of sweet plantain before popping it into her plump mouth.

She chews and swallows, licking her bottom lip before raising a brow at Celia. "Are you staying for the children's hospital gala or…"

"Not this year, Mamita. I'm heading to the Keys in two days. Martica wants to—"

"You're leaving again?" Joaquin interrupts while pushing his own plate away, face pinched tight. "Jesus, Celia. You just got home."

"What home, Joaquin?" She snorts. "My condo?"

"This is your home, and you know it."

"The divorce papers we signed say otherwise."

"Woman, you will send me to an early grave with your stubbornness."

"Remember your children are present," Lionel says then, pushing his chair back to stand, but they're tuning him out while whispering back and forth. There are a few words here and there we all pick up on, *old fool* and *pampered fox* among them—my rebel rolls her eyes while Beatrice fights back a grin. This is their song and dance, and she chooses to let them do their thing. To be honest, I find them amusing if nothing else, and eventually the two stubborn fools will end up together again, which will please my future wife. "I need another beer. Micah?"

Holding mine up, I shake my head at Lionel. "I'm good."

"Be right back, then."

"I could use more wine, son," Celia calls out, but Lionel's already exited the room and she soon gets up to follow. This makes her husband grumble something under his breath, but he's quick to change direction. Now he's speaking to Beatrice and Liliana, but it's my rebel who holds my attention.

She's sitting to my right and rubbing her thigh, fingertips running up and down the length until reaching her knee and starting all over again. They're smooth and tan, flawless skin that I want to bite—brand with my teeth—before licking the abused flesh on my way to her clit. My mouth waters and their conversation becomes background noise, my grip tightening around the bottle in my hand as she giggles at something, and the action causes her body to shift.

There's a little shimmy before she crosses one leg over the other while those lovely tits bounce. *Fuck*, I want to touch her. Claim her.

You don't break your promises. She needs this time.

"…so what do you think, Lili? Want to help your old man for a few months out on the trail?" Joaquin's words pull me out of my thoughts, and I snap my eyes to him. He's looking at her, a big smile on his face. "It'd be just like old times."

Celia chooses that moment to re-enter; one hand holds a topped-up glass and the other a new bottle. She speaks up before I do. "What trail? Are you planning to campaign across the US for another run at being the mayor of Miami?"

"Of course not." Liliana's father gives her a mock glare, yet he's quick to stand and help, taking both items out of Celia's hands before placing them atop the table. Then he retakes his seat, scooting just a little closer to his ex while shifting his attention back to his mildly amused daughter. "Think about it, kiddo. We can be the dream team one more time…at least until I run for state representative. Then we'd be—"

"Dad, I have responsibilities I can't ignore."

"She has a job and school, Joaquin."

"No." Three people speak in unison then—Celia, Liliana, and me —but it's my resounding *no* that shuts down any rebuttal. Years ago when I came to him as a man, I'd been honest and direct. I'd acqui-esce to giving her space to grow and bloom and pursue whatever the fuck makes her happy, but this isn't what she wants. This is another instance where he forgets to think less like a politician and more like a father. His ex-wife glares at him while the son he's groomed to follow in his footsteps opens his mouth to argue, but then quiets when I hold a single hand up. "She's not available, Joaquin, and you know this."

"Micah, it'd only be for a few months. Surely, you can survive without her making your coffee for a little bit."

Silence fills the space at his idiotic remark, belittling everything his amazing daughter does for my company, and I lean forward, my narrowed eyes on his while I lay a palm flat against the table. "Choose your next words wisely, Armas. Liliana is indispensable in my life, and you know it."

"You know I didn't mean it in a bad way, Micah. But I'm her father, and I need—"

"And I'm right here, you know." Her slightly irritated voice cuts through the tension and I sit back, relaxing at the feel of her hand settling on my tense arm and giving it a squeeze. If Rebel's aware of the intimate touch and her effect on me, I have no clue, but it's enough to keep me in my seat and not across the table to wrap my hand around her father's throat.

"Lili, I know school's important and so is your job, but couldn't you—"

"Do you? Because I've already sacrificed, or did you forget the year I took off after high school to help with your last campaign?" Those hazel eyes narrow, lips thinned in a line showing her displeasure. Her tone is accusing, and while I want nothing more than to kick his ass for those remarks, I remain seated and let her deal with her father. *Rebel would be pissed if I touched him.* "Is getting me to agree why you brought us here? Why you took the time to cook all our favorite dishes? To soften us?"

"I wanted you all here..." Joaquin's expression is honest and a little sad; there's no hint of a lie. "...for us to share a meal as a family, no ulterior motive. I swear."

"So you'll respect my wishes, then."

"Si."

"Good, but the answer is a no. I can't." Nothing Joaquin can say to that, and a quick look around the table has everyone staring back at her with pride. Even Beatrice, who's been quiet, shoots her a quick nod. "I'm not a little kid anymore, Dad. School is my life, and my dreams are of graduating top of my class and opening up my own company, something you should understand. You taught us to work hard and smart and not to let anything get in our way; don't ask me to choose again."

Motherfuck, her reply makes me throb beneath the table. That's my girl.

"Okay, Lili. I'm sorry. It won't happen again." He's resigned, but his smile is genuine even if his eyes show longing. There's no hint of anger, and I'm pleased by it. *He misses them but is going about it the wrong way.* "Is it okay to consult with you on some ideas? I promise it won't interfere with your schedule."

"Of course! We can sit down next week if you'd like…maybe over another dinner?"

"It's a date, kiddo."

After that, the conversation around us eases back into talks about the weather and Celia's plans to leave before Saturday and I lean over while they're all occupied. Her scent is always a distraction, but this close and with my lips barely brushing the shell of her ear, I can't hold back my low growl.

"You did good, Rebel. So fucking proud."

Chapter 10
MICAH

My phone vibrates from its place atop my home desk early Friday morning, pulling me away from the current market analysis I've been reading. It's an early morning report sent to me by my broker showing the trajectory for the year and the trending predictions for the second half of 2023. The company's stock is rising at a fast pace, as was to be expected; the current travel trends have outdone the last few years by a large margin, and the deeper into the summer months we get, the higher share profits become.

Yet it all means shit as soon as I press the speaker button after answering. "Speak."

"She's heading toward the office, boss. We'll be there in ten,"

Ligo, her new guard, answers, and from his end, there's the sound of heavy rush-hour traffic. Honking, modified mufflers, and then there's the music—a mixture of Spanish and English that merges into a sound that's uniquely Miami at any time of the day. "Ms. Armas made one stop this morning, and it was to pick up coffee creamer and an assortment of pastries."

Christ, her obsession with coffee and sweets makes me a little jealous.

Does that make me crazy? Absolutely.

Is it rational? Fuck and no.

Truth is, I want her to crave me more than anything in this world. To need me more than the air she breathes.

"Anything else?" Pushing the printed report aside, I move my mouse and bring up the camera feed inside her car. It's one of the few I've added recently to appease me, because the near future holds a drastic change for us. I'm no longer going to trust that she's in an office a few feet from me most of the day, nor will I be complacent with just a few guards to keep her safe.

Rationality loses all meaning when it comes to her. It's my job to worry, not hers.

And I've made moves that will change everything for us.

"She seemed a bit perplexed after receiving a phone call this morning while shopping. Almost annoyed."

On my computer monitor, she's singing and shimmying to music while taking sips from her water cup. That's another of her idiosyncrasies. There's a mug or glass or travel something for every drink and I find the trait utterly adorable, as much as her love for whatever *aesthetically pleasing* means.

"Then I take it that Jeremy canceled?" I'd sent the TA an email after leaving the Armas's home, asking him to meet with me this morning at ten. It's one of the pros of hiring someone from her school and closely connected with her class as part of my IT department.

I give him the false belief that he's of importance in the company.

I move every piece to my benefit. The man's beneath my rebel's intelligence and ethics.

Did she really think I wouldn't find out she was meeting him? That I'd let it slide she went against my wishes?

Not because I'm an asshole or chauvinist—I don't want her mindless acceptance—but because things aren't safe. So far, nothing's turned up on the Diaz men. They're outside of the US, it seems, but the look her brother gave me at dinner bothers me.

That we never got a chance to talk after doesn't help, either.

Lionel was the first one to go after dessert, jumping at the chance to take Beatrice home as she needed to get back and study. She's a nursing student, working toward becoming a pediatric RN, and he wants her even if he's holding back for some unknown reason.

"Ms. Armas did huff that their meeting could be rescheduled for later in the afternoon, but it seems he turned her down. She also reiterated the need for help in choosing her final project."

"Okay." *I'll allow it next week.* "Keep everyone out of our floor until Monday unless I'm there. No excuse. I'll be there soon."

"Understood, Mr. Royce."

Hanging up, I sit back and watch her maneuver through traffic. She has a little bit of a lead foot. Something I'm guilty of myself, but where I'm a hot head, Liliana is careful in her madness, and it takes her those ten minutes exactly to arrive and slip into her personal parking space beside mine. Her rose gold Mercedes Benz shuts off and the driver door opens, revealing a pair of stilettos that have me biting my bottom lip.

It's a small obsession I've noticed as of late from her.

Not that she didn't wear *please bend me over* heels before, but these latest additions are quite a punishment for my cock. I want to have her greet me at the door to our home while wearing nothing but those shoes. I want to feel the metal buckles dig into the skin of my back and sides as I fuck her into the mattress of our bed.

Rebel's door closes on the screen, and a second later she's out of my line of sight until I switch to the garage's security system. I follow her from the elevator up to our floor and then inside her office where she settles in while quickly setting up the computer system behind her. On the large monitor, there's a fast sequence of letters and symbols running and Liliana watches the screen with interest, head tilted to the side, and more so when a certain code appears and everything freezes.

She's quick to attack her keyboard, fingers flying across it, but I can't quite catch the expression on her face until she turns. The system is rebooting and her brows are furrowed, lips thinned right before she says *what the fuck*, and I'm out the door and reaching my car minutes after.

"Buenos Dias, Ms. Armas," I say from her doorway, and it's the first time I think I've truly caught her off guard. Since clocking in, her attention's been on the monitors, pinging back and forth while chewing on her cherry-pink bottom lip. This morning, they're shiny with her favorite lip gloss—begging to be bitten.

At the sound of my voice, her eyes dart up and my favorite reaction crests over her. Liliana shivers for me; it's small and almost undiscernible, but there isn't a single thing about this woman that I'm not attuned to. I can make out the smallest change or shift, and enjoy the way her nipples tighten behind the thin fabric of her bra.

She doesn't like padded coverage.

She chooses pretty and delicate with touches of sheerness, and they all drive me wild.

I can make out the tiny flower patterns on this one behind one of my favorite looks on her—a delicate polka-dot wrap dress with a belt around her waist to accentuate her curves. It has a little frill, ends right above her knees, and on her feet are the shoes with the provocative hardware that I need to see up close.

"Stand up, Rebel."

"W-What?"

"Stand. Up."

"Okay." Slowly, she pushes away from her desk and walks around it without me having to further prompt. Rebel stops with her ass perched against the edge, hands on either side of her while I take a moment to get my fill. From her blood-red painted toes to her long legs and then the peek of cleavage, this woman is the physical definition of feminine beauty, but it's her heart that makes her perfect.

Liliana loves hard. Sometimes more than she should.

"Come here."

"Micah, what's going on?" Apart from the way she looks at me, the attraction she fights hard not to show, there's a tightness around her eyes I don't like. Something is stressing her. "Did something happen?"

"No." And because I need her just as much, I close the distance between us and yank her to me by the belt around her waist before wrapping my arms around her much smaller frame. At first she's surprised, emitting a small squeal that I find utterly adorable before relaxing in my hold. To an outsider, this is an innocent hug between friends—I've never hidden just how close our families are—but to me, it's taking care of what's mine. "This is because you need it, sweetheart."

"How did you know?" It's muffled by my shirt. Unconsciously she's nuzzling my chest, but I don't call her out on it.

"Because I stalk your every move." It's the truth, but she finds it funny and snorts before smacking my arm. "Don't believe me?"

"Sure." A slim finger pokes my stomach, making me jump, but I don't release her yet. Instead, I flex my right hand over her ribs and begin to tap a random rhythm. The threat of retaliation is there, and she knows it. "Don't you dare."

"Then apologize, Rebel."

"Nothing to...okay! Okay!" With a breathless giggle, she

squirms against me while my fingers press in a little deeper. "I'm sorry. There."

"Try being a little nicer."

"Fine." Pulling back enough that I can see her face, she pouts her lips and bats her lashes. Both acts are subtle and coquettish, but what I adore the most is how for a second she watches my mouth with rapt hunger. How her hazel eyes darken and she gives her head a small shake before wrapping the two-toned evergreen tie around her slim fingers. Now I'm the one being yanked, pulled until I'm forced to bend without fully releasing her, and our faces are inches apart. Her exhale is my inhale; I follow her every movement as if it were my religion and the way her lips curve into a sweet smile before kissing my cheek. "I'm sorry, Captain Grumps. Promise to be on my best behavior today."

Motherfuck, my cock is solid as a rock the second her soft mouth touches my skin, but the way I throb at her soft tone and the use of a nickname I've come to love has me stepping away. Not by much, just enough that I'm not digging my cock into her abdomen; even with heels, she's petite in comparison to my six-four frame.

"Feel better?"

"A little."

"Want to tell me why you looked so stressed when I walked in?" I ask, and immediately Liliana begins to tense, but I tsk. "Quit that, or I'll send you home."

"You wouldn't dare."

I pinch her chin. "Try me."

"You're being mean today, Micah." My reply to that is an arched brow. "It's probably nothing, but—"

"Does it have something to do with the programs you're running?" My eyes leave her face and look over her shoulder, trying to make sense of the fast binary code now running across each of her screens. And while I'm not an expert in this field, I do understand that what she's doing right now is outside our protocol. "What did you find, Rebel?"

"That's the problem. Nothing." Pulling away from me, she walks back around her desk and leans over to get a better read of the screen while I follow. I'm standing just a few feet from her, eyes trailing down her back while my chest expands on a deep breath. *Fuck, she's gorgeous. Smells so good.* "...this is all too clean. Even while running our scans and enforcing firewalls or even a simple mainte- nance upgrade, there's always a trace of human error." That pulls me from my thoughts and I focus on her words, but more importantly, where she's pointing. Different areas on each monitor are in bright red, the sequences flying across while she tuts. "Nothing is ever this clean. Be it someone hit the wrong key then backspaced or an employee visited a website they shouldn't be on during company hours, a trail is always left behind indicating the source, but your systems are running as if out of the box. A first-time setup versus years of data."

"What are you thinking?"

"Someone cleaned the servers recently but was smart enough to erase their walkthrough. I can't find any log-ins." Looking back at me from over her shoulder, she purses her lips. "It's frustrating the hell out of me to figure it out, but I will. There's always a pathway."

"What do you need from me?" If there's someone in this world I trust, it's Liliana. She'd never betray me. So, I'll let her hunt while I watch her back—kill whoever tries to stop her because I don't believe in coincidences.

A theft at her mother's condo.

Two idiots on my ship attempting to do the same.

Her father declined Diaz of a huge real estate deal.

"I need control of your servers for a few hours tonight. No one can be here or touch anything."

"Done. Is that a new program?"

"It's mine. I built it." A blush spreads across the apple of her cheeks. "Thought about using it as part of my final project, but I'm not sure. Jeremy thinks I need to focus on removing and retrieving files as that's something my professor—"

"Fuck that." *My gorgeous little genius.* "I believe in it."

"Really? Just like that?" She gives me a look that holds surprise, but I simply bop her nose with the tip of a finger. *Silly girl.* "What if I'm wrong or—"

"I trust you."

"You do?"

"Always."

Tension drains from her and she turns to face me, her smile sweet. "Thank you so much for saying that, Micah. I was worried you'd think I was overstepping or making something up. I'd never do anything to hurt you or Royce Cruise Lines—never—but after we talked, something about it kept bugging me." A dainty hand raises and her slim fingers reach for my hand, giving it a squeeze. "Whatever is going on, I'll help you stop it."

And because I can't help myself, I give a short tug and the hand still gripping mine moves her back into my personal space. I don't hug her this time, but I do lower my lips and place a kiss to her forehead, lingering a bit so I can breathe her in. So sweet. A decadent cake.

"Do what you must. You have my backing," I speak against her fragrant skin. "Guards will be here to secure the building while you work."

"I'll be here late tonight. Past midnight, though."

"And I'll make sure our dinner is delivered at six. Finish what you're doing now and go home and rest. It's going to be a long night." Turning before she can protest, I walk away but then pause near her doorway, remembering something. "Can you get a hold of Lionel before you leave? Ask him to come by after two if possible."

"I can't." She sounds surprised.

"And why is that?"

"Didn't he tell you? They left this morning for Tallahassee."

Chapter 11
MICAH

∞♥

Watching her in her element is the definition of sexual foreplay.

This beautiful girl with those big doe eyes and plump lips is staring at the screens before her, teeth digging into her bottom lip as she concentrates. It's been that way for a while now. She reads something that makes her brows pinch tight and then types a command using the Bluetooth keyboard before tilting her head to the side and then starting all over again.

Moreover, I have the urge to walk over and kiss her forehead and then her lips.

Eat her pussy until she explodes on my tongue and then put her to bed.

"She's utterly delectable," I groan low, but my little rebel doesn't so much as twitch. If anything, she purses her lips and then moves to another large CPU a few feet from us, tugging over one of her large stands with a monitor and plugging it into the front port. "I could help you with that, Liliana."

"No need." That's it. I'm dismissed, and if I didn't find everything about her adorable, I'd be offended. Then, there's the maddening way what she's wearing affects me: plain black tights, a sweatshirt with her school's logo in the front, and Nikes on her feet. Simple. Comfortable. Downright sinful while the dark waves I want to run my fingers through are in a messy top knot that I have no idea how she's keeping in place with a pen. "But I *could* use a coffee."

I'm hard. Balls swollen. But the most frustrating thing is how little attention she's paying me.

Rebel's lost in her work, her eyes skimming through the lines of code, running between two large monitors she's attached to stands. When she first brought them in, I'd been unsure of them, but I saw the use after wheeling the mobile units into the room before stepping aside so she could attach her cords.

The servers for my company are on the ground floor near the back end of the building, and she needed to be close while running her security check. It's silent in the room outside of the sound of built-in fans whirling to keep the equipment cool.

That's all I've been allowed to do. Now I watch and admire.

"Is that so?" I arch a brow at her disregard and then take in the small quirk of those plump lips into a cute grin. "I've been relegated to assistant duties?"

"Not necessarily." This time the grin becomes a smirk while the process starts all over again as she plugs in a couple of commands, then watches the sequence without moving. We're almost done with all the units in this room, having gone through them one by one, and when I asked her why she didn't use the administrative system, she rolled her eyes before answering. *So they know I'm on to them? Your team is good, Micah, and I'm not about making things easier for those crooked fuckers.* "But maybe one of the guards is a barista in his off time and he can help curb my craving at…" Rebel looks down at her smartwatch, her eyes widening "…two in the morning! No wonder I'm starting to crash a bit."

"We can stop if you want. You've done a lot already." The firm set of her jaw told me she didn't agree with my suggestion, much like I'll never let anyone take care of her needs. It's my job to meet all of her wishes, even if it's something as simple as a cup of coffee. "Fine. I'll be back in a few minutes with your addiction. Don't leave this room."

"Thank you, Micah." Leaving her equipment, she takes the few steps separating us and gives a tiny jump to kiss my chin. "You're the best."

"I know." Leaving her to it, I tap one of the machines before walking out of the room. Ligo and Isaac are standing in the lobby while a few of my most trusted have set up posts around the building. No one is allowed in or out without my consent. Every company employee has been sent home, though, and that includes the night shift security staff.

I want no one aware of what she's doing. Let the rats stew in their filth.

Most were happy about this, but I noticed the reaction of a few who seemed perturbed.

The IT department had scheduled maintenance for tonight, but I forced them to cancel.

No reason was given. No heads up.

But it's Jeremy's face that stood out the most. That, and the older male who came with him under the pretense of delivering an unscheduled presentation, the latter of which dragged an ancient rolling cart with everything needed for this pitch.

"You wanted to see me, Mr. Royce?" Jeremy steps into my office, taking a seat across from me after I wave him in. He's an average man. Nothing special about his lanky build or face, and the employee accompanying him is no different.

Both are standing just inside the threshold looking behind them every few seconds as if searching for something. Or someone.

"Take a seat, please." My eyes shift to the other man, who I don't recall ever seeing before, nor was he invited to this meeting. *"And you are?"*

"Ummm..." He swallows hard while Jeremy taps his thigh in a nervous manner. *"Sorry, sir. I'm Jessie—"*

"Jessie what?"

"Jessie Dunlap."

"Hmmm." I don't say anything else for a minute, letting them sweat it out. I'd brought Jeremy here today not just to keep Liliana from meeting him, but as a team leader, he needs to shut down tonight's scheduled maintenance. *"What's the relationship between you two?"*

"He's my older brother," Jeremy speaks up; I take in the nervous tilt in his tone.

"And why is your older brother here, Mr. Dunlap?"

"He works here?" It's stated as a question, and I keep my expression neutral. Strike one; I didn't hire this man. I'm involved in every facet of new hires, including the initial and then entry interview a month into employment. The same goes for after they leave the company.

"Since when?"

"I don't understand the question."

"Then let me dumb it down." Beside me, I have a cup of coffee with hazelnut creamer prepared the way Liliana likes it, and I take a sip. Sugary and foamy and everything I hate, but fuck me if I don't drink it down because it's how she takes hers. And after watching her make it this way for so long, I've become an expert at matching her recipe. *"I didn't hire him, Jeremy. Who did, and when?"*

"Liliana said you approved of my bringing him in as a consultant a few months back. Around February...was she wrong?"

That's the second lie. Rebel has no problem telling me where to go and how fast to get there, so talking to me about a potential *employee she'd find beneficial for her team is nothing she'd pussy-foot around with. Hell, when she spoke of Jeremy, it was with confidence. Knowing I needed a new head of department in her field, she approached me and expressed respect for two people in her class:*

Jeremy Dunlap and Samantha Cintek. However, the female student was poached early on by a large airline company based out of South Florida, leaving behind the teacher's assistant.

"I must've forgotten. My apologies." Sitting back, I look at them and wait. Silence ensues. Not so much as a peep until a phone pings, and it's mine. On the screen, I see the text but don't reply.

Ms. Armas is home and safe. ~Ligo

"No problem, sir. It was a simple mistake." This comes from Jessie, and I nod. Let him think whatever he wants. The older Dunlap doesn't pick up on my annoyance and neither does Jeremy, but they quickly shift into trying to show me a newly developed security program. They have a slide, a folder with a pitch, and the risk factors for something untried outside of their experimental runs at home.

Jessie is standing and ready to start, excited to get my ear, but I hold a hand up. "You're here because there's been a change of plans and I need your help."

That bothers Jeremy, and annoyance flashes in his eyes but he is quick to control it. "Of course. My apologies, Mr. Royce. How can I be of service?"

"Cancel anything your department's running tonight. I want everything shut down before six."

"What! Why?" Jeremy exclaims, standing up and swallowing hard. His hands are also clenching. "Why are you—"

"Is there a problem?" My eyes narrow, taking in every minute shift the two idiots make. Then, there's the nervous twitch in his right eye. "Are you unable to follow simple orders?"

"No, sir. It's just that things like that take time." Voice low. Contrite. "Is there a specific reason as to why—"

"You work for me," I grit out, jaw ticking as I fight to control my anger. His behavior is pissing me off, and right now isn't the time to break his jaw and then watch him swallow his front teeth. Although, the sight would be satisfying. *"I do not need to give you an explanation. Do as I say."*

"Of course. It'll be done." Jessie stands after answering for his brother, too. His head gives a small bow before placing a hand on Jeremy's arm and giving it a quick squeeze. *"We'll get on that right away, Mr. Royce."*

I called Isaac as soon as both men exited my office.

Their behavior didn't sit right with me and I want them investigated. But more than that, it's how they kept glancing toward Liliana's office as they walked toward the elevator.

Nervous. Shifty. Paranoid.

I won't speak to her about her TA's behavior yet; I need proof first, but I'll be watching him like a hawk.

Turning off the frother, I test the foam's taste and nod, knowing she'll like this. It takes me minutes to serve everything to her liking, even going as far as using a tray to carry her coffee and a few of the gourmet cookies I'd ordered for her as a dessert. In her rush to get downstairs and start, Liliana forgot about them, but I know she'll appreciate the gesture now.

Heading downstairs, I ride the elevator down and then walk back to where I left her. She's at the last machine and frowning, but before I can ask her what's wrong, I get a phone call.

Her brother's name flashes across the screen, and I pick up after the third ring. Not that he waits for me to say anything—he's breathing hard while the sound of heavy rain comes from the other side of the line.

"We need to meet. I'll be in Orlando in a few hours." The line goes dead right after and I'm left watching my girl, who's still oblivious to my presence. And it's not until after I hang up that she turns my way, face wary and exhausted.

"Everything okay, Micah?"

"You found something?" I ask instead, shifting the attention away from Lionel's call.

"I think I did."

"But?"

"I need more time before making any type of accusation."

"Okay." Stepping closer to her, I hand over her late-night snack and then lean down to lay a kiss at the edge of her mouth. Close, but still not what we both need. "Finish up and head home. Ligo will take you back."

"My car's here." She's a little breathy. A little flushed. "There's no need—"

"Ligo will take you home. Please don't argue with me on this."

"Okay."

"Thank you."

I'm gone a few minutes later. Her brother's urgency didn't sit well with me, and after giving her guard strict instructions to stay stationed outside her building until I get back, I slip inside my car. Isaac gets in the passenger side, always loyal, and we are on our way to Central Florida within minutes.

Everything that's been happening keeps replaying in my head as I get on the Turnpike.

The idea that my rebel could be hurt physically or emotionally stands against everything I am as her man. No matter what, I'll protect her, and I think it's time things change between us.

And I'll start by making sure she's always within my reach.

Chapter 12
LILIANA

The sudden knock on the front door pulls my attention away from the true-crime docu-series I started watching a few hours ago. I've been sucked into a vortex, unable to pull my attention away from the hot mess on the screen, the newest retelling of a serial killer's journey from the '70s through the early '90s in the US.

This time they've made it into more of a show format, going through each of the main events—murders—he committed through his Midwest trail of horror. So far, each one is more gruesome than the last, and I'm questioning my sanity for watching this.

It's scary how you never truly know a person. Not really.

Pressing pause on the remote, I tilt my head in the direction of the entrance while taking a quick sip of my coffee. It's laced with a tiny smidge of bourbon, a scent I associate with Micah—one that's embedded into the clothes I wore two days ago when we spent most of the night at Royce Cruise Lines—at least until he disappeared without much of an explanation.

A phone call and he was out the door, only pausing long enough to demand I let a man named Ligo drive me home.

Once again, I find myself missing him, and I bring the sweatshirt I'd worn Friday night up to my face. It fills me with a piece of him, smells so good, and I can't help the little moan that slips past my lips. "I'm weak when it comes to him. Look at what I did to my coffee."

This yearning is a dangerous thing, and because of it, I've created a bit of sacrilege with my caffeinated drink today just to get a tiny taste of him. To have the scent of bourbon, light as it is, fill my nose and complement the real thing that still clings to my clothes.

I'm surrounding myself with him.

Almost feels like I'm nesting like they do in those romance books I love to read.

Pushing those thoughts from my mind, I tilt my head while listening for more noise, yet silence follows the previous interruption. For a few seconds, I look at the screen. It's the episode where he claims the life of his third victim, and I'm left staring into the eyes of the killer whose hand is raised with a weapon held above the next victim's head.

Nothing. Not another sound.

And it's moments like these, while I watch something that makes me a little jumpy, that I wish my mother had a front door surveillance system. At the very least, a peephole camera, since the woman was gone faster than I blinked. *Then again, everyone in the family has been radio silent for days now.*

"Mother trucker!" I scream then, jumping when the killer finally swings the weapon in his hand and the blow cracks the victim's skull wide open, blood and other matter squirting out. Another blow and the murderer groans in pleasure, sexualizing the moment as every-thing around them turns crimson red. The sight brings a story I heard on the news to mind for some reason and I swallow hard, eyes shifting toward the door and back again.

A man killed his neighbor over a game of cards inside the home's garage—both had been drinking—and the latter in a fit of rage beat his friend's head in with a hammer. Because monsters have always blended in seamlessly within their society. And the more shows like this give us an insight into how the mind of a killer thinks, I'm a firm believer that they never truly hid, but we're just unobservant.

Because we don't see past what's in front of us. Too consumed by a false reality.

We're groomed to focus on what fits the narrative we need at the moment and for our personal gains.

It's how those unafraid to break the law survive.

They blend. Become friends and build bonds with those in their close circles. And while these thoughts roam my head, I'm left wondering who the hell is at my door.

Someone knocked. I'm not going crazy. "I'm not expecting anyone."

It's the weekend, and I'm off. I'd planned to spend my Sunday as I am—curled up while being lazy—surrounded by nothing but junk food and my latest Starbucks order that I doctored. The venti cold brew with sweet vanilla foam has made me smile since the moment it arrived, while the copious amounts of cheese danishes accompa-nying it have probably wiped the location out for the day.

Then, there's the way the show has kept me from changing out of the spandex shorts and loose-fitting tank top I'd slipped into after my quick morning shower. It's all about comfort and gore today.

It's also a reminder of how I failed to get a quick morning run in, but the urge to burn off some of the nervous energy currently residing in me didn't appeal after I got a peek at this drama's trailer.

Because it's been building. Today's all about affirmations and forgiveness, both of these starting and ending with admitting my feelings about Micah's confusing behavior toward me lately. The praises and small touches—how he defended me against my father—and it's messing with my head.

I know it's me. How I want to see the possibility of a *more* where there isn't one, but tell that to my needy heart.

His trust in me makes my chest swell with pride. The kiss he gave me on my forehead after I explained my concerns, and the following smile right after—I've claimed as mine even if he doesn't see me that way—make me feel special and I'm clinging to it. Shamelessly so.

Pay attention, chica. Someone's outside.

"Maybe it's a mistake. They knocked on the wrong door." Yet the moment I'm done speaking, another sharp rap sounds. This one is louder than the last, canceling my idea of a wrong condo being the cause, and I pull the blankets off before lowering my legs. I'm a bit stiff as I do this and reach both hands up to stretch, the slight burn of muscle feeling great after a few hours of cuddling my blankets and sweatshirt. "I blame the app for my lack of movement today. That's my story and I'm sticking to their addictiveness."

"Ms. Armas!" is suddenly called out followed by a persistent ringing of the doorbell. "Ms. Armas!"

"What the hell?" I mutter to myself while narrowing my eyes and padding over. I'm not dumb enough to just open the door even though this building has great security—especially not after the deep rabbit hole I've fallen into with this series—but on the other side of the viewer, I find a woman with her raised hand poised to knock again. There's more than one, actually, and they're all wearing a company shirt I'm all too familiar with.

Without hesitating this time, I open the door. Yet right as I open my mouth to ask them what's going on, they enter my mother's condo and head deeper into the house without missing a beat. It's as if they know the layout, and I'm left standing with the words *"can I help you"* sitting on the tip of my tongue.

They don't look at me, though. Nor do they introduce themselves. Instead, their sights are set on my unpacked boxes and what sounds to be the luggage in my room I'd transferred over from my father's house during the move. My plans were to show him that I'm okay with being alone and then get a place of my own, far away from the constant politically made moves or the mandated family social appearances.

I love my family. Truly do.

Yet sometimes it all gets to be too much. The stress. The feelings of being alone.

Like now, Mom's in Key West doing *her* while my father and brother are off playing golf and then having dinner with the governor, and I worry Dad will back out of his promise. The city needs funds to restore damaged beach-front commercial property, while one of his biggest donors is asking for a favor.

Or better yet, cashing in what he perceives as owed to him.

Rodolfo Diaz and his associates want the rights to purchase a state-owned park, bypassing any red tape, and while the mayor of Miami isn't the deciding vote, his friendship with the governor could pave the way. But that's politics for you. One hand washes the other and eventually those back end *I owe yous* often become multimillion—sometimes billion—dollar deals.

Something falls inside the bedroom I'm occupying. The heavy thud has me almost following, but before I can, or demand answers, he walks in.

Always him. Always so handsome.

Dressed in a pair of white chino shorts with a corded tan belt and a light blue linen shirt, Micah looks like walking perfection as he steps into the foyer. Like a model for any high-fashion magazine, he owns the room with both sleeves rolled up to his elbows—exposing his detailed tattooed sleeve— and I find him utterly panty-destroying.

My mouth waters and core clenches.

There's something so uniquely attractive about a man with tattoos. More so when his attention is on me. There's a smile on his face and a tiny hint of challenge in his eyes, both of which leave me without the ability to demand anything:

Answers.

His touch.

That everyone but *him* leave.

"Ready to go, Rebel?"

"Go? Go where?" This leaves me on a high pitch, and I clear my throat, forcing myself to find the painting on the wall to the right of his head simply fascinating. It's a large piece depicting beauty and self-confidence; a woman whose face is half-covered by delicate yet bold flowers that flow across her flawless skin while depicting pure, raw beauty.

It's gorgeous. So emotive and brings forth this sense of inner strength—of finding your own worth away from societal standards— yet right now, I can't acknowledge anything but the butterflies currently taking flight inside of me. They flutter beneath my skin; my nerves are so unsettled I nearly sway but manage to brace a hand against the closest piece of furniture and grip the entry table's edge as he steps into my personal space.

"With me." His hand pries mine before giving it a tug just hard enough that I'm forced to turn his way, seconds before I'm led toward the bedroom I'm using. There's a flurry of movement inside, his female employees boxing everything that isn't of my personal use while the older of the trio zips up the largest of the unpacked suit-cases while being careful not to touch anything inside. And while I'm busy trying to make heads or tails of what I'm seeing, Micah moves to take his place slightly behind me. Close, yet there's a respectable distance. "I'm taking you home, Liliana."

"Home." The word is breathy yet infused with every bit of the confusion I'm teetering on. "I am home."

"No. You're not." His exhale teases the sensitive flesh just below my ear, his body bent low enough that his cheek is almost pressed against mine. "I'll replace whatever they don't pack."

"Micah, you're not—"

"Remove everything as I've instructed." Within seconds of that order, my possessions are taken out of the condo by men who only appeared after the women exited. Out of all the people who've been here, I recognize two and neither Ligo nor Isaac make eye contact.

His personal guards never do. They are always around, someone as rich as Micah needing protection—hell, even my father has some security—but they're seldom seen.

Yet Ligo drove me home two days ago. Made sure I got inside safely.

They work quickly. No words are exchanged; I do nothing more than watch as his employees remove every trace of my living here—everything but my underwear or the clean clothes inside of a hamper I'd yet to put away. It all disappears before the front door closes behind the last person's exit.

Moreover, I'm not upset by it.

Confused? Yes.

A little turned on by his dominance? Without a doubt.

But I also have to admit that I've done little with what I've brought into this condo. I've just been coasting by while Mom travels and the rest of my family works. I keep busy with work and school and the few friends I have, but this isn't a place I'd miss if I were to move.

Not really.

And If I'm honest with myself, this place feels like a hotel. Pretty yet missing that lived-in feel that brings comfort.

I knew that coming in, so it's not a shocker to me, and it's one of the reasons I've been living out of my suitcase, just taking out what I need at any given time. Instead of filling the empty drawers or closet shelves, I re-stuff what I'm done using back into my luggage or a box.

Only my work clothes are hung, and I consider that done out of a necessary practicality.

"I'll help you with the rest," Micah says, pulling me away from my thoughts. It's almost as if reality slips into my consciousness with the weight of a battering ram, forcing me to realize that he's taking me away from here. That I didn't stop anyone from touching my belongings or that I'm not questioning his motives.

Instead, I flick my eyes to him and take in the way his muscles flex as he moves past me and picks up my hamper, tucking in my lavender-colored tights that are close to falling out. Then, there's the way his fingers touch the matching sports bra and a nearly see-through tank I wear to bed sometimes. The pads skim over each item, quickly and without any expression on his face, but to me, it's a contact I feel from the tips of my toes to my now hard nipples.

Yet it's when he walks to the dresser and reaches for the bag from a boutique I discovered by chance on Biscayne Boulevard. that I react. I'm over to him in a second and slapping his hand away, blushing at the fact he almost fingered the small bits of lace and mesh and satin that I feel sexy in.

"Sorry..." my cheeks feel as though they are on fire "...I'll get these myself."

"You have five minutes to do so." Voice deeper. A bit rougher, and when I meet his eyes again there's something in them I've never seen before. It flares and dominates the pupils, expanding them until very little of the blue irises I love is left. "Don't keep me waiting, Rebel. I'll be right outside."

A warning. A hidden threat to come back and pack me himself, and knowing that my cheeks are heated—the blush feels as though it's traveling from my face to neck and lower—all I can manage is a nod.

Which seems to be enough because without another word he steps out of the room, and a whooshing breath leaves me. Everything is happening so fast. Unpredictable.

Did something happen that I'm not aware of?

And while a normal person would run after him and demand an explanation, I begin to pack up the little bit that's still here. My underwear, a handful of clothes, and my journal that's been sitting on the bedside table since the morning after my last entry.

My guess is I brought it with me before falling into the bed.

It takes minutes for me to wrap it up and exit, nearly bumping into Micah who's leaning against the opposite wall. He doesn't say anything, but his expression is pleased. More so when I let him lead me out the front door and straight toward the elevator while two locksmiths change the old deadbolt to a modern number combination system.

Chapter 13
MICAH

I never made it to Orlando in the early morning hours on Saturday.

Not Sunday.

Not Monday either.

Yet, I did manage to bring Liliana one step closer to living with me. There are only two penthouses on this floor, and no one knows they're connected by a small hallway that leads from my closet to hers. I want it that way. This is backup insurance in case of an emergency, and with the position her father has unknowingly put them in, I'm glad I thought to do so.

The area is wider than an average hallway and is dimly lit. On one side, there are floor-to-ceiling windows, while on the opposite side I have pictures of her throughout the years. From when we met, right up to her last birthday, they highlight each milestone, her smile, and the way she turned from a sassy teen to a stunning woman before my eyes, but my favorite will always be the ones of us together.

Family shared Christmases.

Days spent out on the beach.

Every fucking special moment that matters.

And one day soon, I'll show her these. Gift her the proof of just how much I've obsessed and waited—always loved her but giving her room to grow while protecting her from the horrors of our world. Because our lives will never be normal. We walk a fine line between crime and nobility while embracing the inevitability of spilling the enemies' blood.

A few more feet, and I'm inside her private quarters via a moveable storage unit meant to house her shoes. A hidden door: this little arrangement lets me come and go as I please, and right now, I'm pleased by the sight that greets me atop the oversized white ottoman at the center. Tufted and in a soft fabric, her clothes from today are strewn across it, the only mess in the space while the rest is neatly organized by color and fabric. She's unpacked and made herself at home.

No more boxes. No more living out of her luggage.

The tight, high-waisted skirt with buttons running down the left side along with her top, a cap-sleeved light pink number, is soft beneath my fingertips. I skim them across each item. Slowly savoring; I breathe in deep as her cupcake scent infiltrates my senses and bathes me in warmth. It fills and settles me. It helps me relax after a stressful day, and it further cements how much I truly love this woman.

Every part of her. Always only her.

Moving each piece aside, I bite my bottom lip as her lingerie is next.

Peach-colored and lace, the bra is delicate with sheer cups that don't hide a damn thing. Her nipples—such lovely little tight tips—

have been playing with my control all day. During our quick mid-morning coffee date, they beaded for me. In the afternoon when she dropped off a merchandising report with the mock-ups for a new line of loungewear and souvenirs, they'd been highlighted by the sunshine coming through my office floor-to-ceiling windows.

I could almost make out their exact shade. How tight they get in my presence.

And there was the thin, crisscrossing pattern just below the underwire of her bra in the same material that ties together in a bow mid-abdomen. It's sexy. Exquisite. And the matching bottoms are even more tempting.

"*Christ*, Rebel." This couldn't be called underwear. Not with how tiny and fragile the gusset meant to cover her cunt is. Indecent is what it should be called, and fuck, if I'm not hard.

I'm throbbing. Jerking behind the fabric of my joggers as I bring her thong up to my nose and inhale, groaning when I find a little bit of wetness at the center. Just a bit, but it's enough to have me tugging my pants low enough to free my cock.

I grip myself tight as I run the tip of my tongue across the lace. Stroke my dick up and down roughly as the pure sweetness of her pussy overtakes my senses. I'm fucking my fist while she sleeps just a few feet from where I stand inside her walk-in, unleashing my lust while the cause and need isn't aware of just how fucking close the devil plays to his princess.

"But it will never be enough, Liliana. Nothing short of the day you wear my ring will settle me." Closing my eyes, I pick up my pace. Each brutal tug is near angry; I've been denying myself for so long—sacrificed what I wanted to give her what she needs—but the time to collect what I've earned is near. *Almost.*

Pumping my hips to that thought, I take another deep lungful of her scent in its most natural form.

Sweet. Decadent. Pure.

It sits on the tip of my tongue, and I can't stop myself from imagining the day I eat her cunt for the first time. How soft and wet she'll be as I grip her thighs while holding her in place, licking every drop of her slick heat. How she'll tremble beneath me as I feel her tiny hole clench—trying to get any part of me inside of her while I slide the fat of my tongue through her labia.

"Fuck. Fucking hell, baby," I hiss out through clenching teeth, coming into my hand as I bite down on the almost nonexistent lace. It further ignites me, her scent and that tiny bit of wetness controlling each snap of my hips and the painful grip on my girth.

My release hits hard and messy. It spills and slips, falling onto her clothes and the edge of the ottoman, pulling a satisfied grin from me. I have no shame, nor do I care. Instead, I'm filled with animalistic pride at marking my territory.

Because she is just that. Motherfucking mine.

Leaving her clothing as is, all except her underwear, I exit her closet and straight into her bedroom. My angel is sleeping, face down and with one leg raised, which only serves to angle her ass up. It's round and accentuated by the thin sheet covering her small body atop the king-size bed—an exact replica to mine—I bought for her.

My eyes travel around the room, and I'm pleased to see traces of her everywhere.

Where her mother's condo didn't hold any personalized touches that showed she lived there, this space has pictures, an obscene amount of fluffy, decorative pillows, and smells like her.

Sugary sweet. Decadent.

Then, there's the journal beside her on the nightstand. A familiar sight that pulls a smile from me, and I don't hesitate when I cross the room and pick it up. The black and gold notebook has quite a few entries, but as I flip through the pages, I don't find anything new from the days after I carried her to bed last week.

She'd drank that night after enjoying the dinner I'd sent her and then called me. It was a little slurred and cute; she'd given me a command and then hung up before I could make any promises.

Someday, I want to get married on a beach, Micah. Make it happen.

That day, I'd been hard before she ever hung up. I'd been throbbing when I unlocked her mother's front door using the emergency key given to me by Celia before Liliana moved in, finding my pretty rebel fast asleep on the couch.

Her family knows of my intentions; I've never hidden them, nor do I mask my emotions behind the guise of being Lionel's best friend. He comes second to her, and that will never change.

The TV was still on when I let myself in, displaying the *are you still watching* question most apps flash when you've been watching a series for a few hours. At some point during the evening, Liliana started a Spaniard show about bank robbers and then conked out.

I took her to bed and tucked her in, then sat down on an oversized chair right in the corner. That's something she's always had inside her room—a big and comfy soft seat to curl up and read in, and I made sure the one in my penthouse was right across from where she lies and within the perfect viewing range.

It's close enough to appease me as I watch her sleep. Calms me as I pull out the pen she keeps tucked into the spirals of her latest journal and write an entry of my own on the very last page.

It's a promise to protect, love, and honor.

To get her father out of the mess he's in, and after reading through the files Alfred handed over, I know how to pull the Diaz men from the hole they've crawled into. Rodolfo's obsession is his downfall, but so is his stupidity.

He's digging to find a way to force Joaquin's compliance and by using his family, I've been made a part of the solution. By going against me—hiring men to find dirt on my company to force my father to add pressure—I've become his biggest enemy.

I'm coming for him.

One day soon, I will give you the wedding of your dreams.

Micah.

Meet me in downtown Tampa on Thursday. Ten p.m. by the docks. ~Lionel

THAT'S IT. We haven't talked since his frantic phone call and then cancellation, but then again, I've been busy myself. The information he left atop my desk held plenty to sift through, but it's the combination for Celia's safe that made the difference. She hides secrets well.

Foreign bank accounts.

Favors owed.

The ties to a criminal family I'm all too familiar with.

The De Leons are well known in Miami and throughout the state, but even I didn't know that Thiago's mother and Joaquin are cousins. Not close, but the relation could jeopardize the picture-perfect image his constituents have of him.

A mayor and a well-run cartel don't bode well for his state representative aspirations, although the silent favor he did for Thiago a few years back—giving him the access to legally purchase a section of the port—would ruin him. It's information like this that Rodolfo and son want, and they almost had it.

"Why the fuck would he leave something like this in Celia's care?"

The answer is stupidity. Too trusting in his position.

Power comes, but not all can maintain their tight leash on it. Someone's always vying for your position—no one is completely safe—and this is ammunition for piss stains who could care less if they hurt someone when the end goal is all that matters.

Placing everything back inside my home vault, a reinforced steel room hidden behind a wall-sized painting of my rebel that holds my weapons and important information, I grab a Glock and exit. I'm tempted to check on her before she heads off to start her day, to open one of the many cameras throughout her home installed for my pleasure, but I don't.

Instead, I walk out of my home and meet the eyes of a man a few feet from me guarding this floor. A few are spread throughout the premises, each one taking an entry point or access—a path that could lead to her. Her father's enemies are stupid enough to try. His children have become fair game by association, and the De Leon name isn't one to take lightly.

My money is on Rodolfo knowing and needing proof.

Ligo is quick to slide the keycard across the panel of the elevator, opening the private lift that only she and I have access to unless it's an emergency.

I've upped security to four guards, who for the time being live and secure this high-rise at all times. They alternate shifts while occupying the entire floor beneath us. They are never seen but always there.

But more importantly, there are only two units on this level:

She lives in one. I watch her from the other.

"Boss," Ligo says, his head bowed as I pass and enter. "Everything's ready for her ride to the university and then to the office. We'll keep her safe."

"You better. Not a hair out of place."

"Yes, sir. I'll keep you updated."

I give him a nod in response and head down and straight into my parking space near the elevator bank. Isaac is already there and my car is on, leaving me to slip inside the back while he remains behind the wheel.

Traffic is a little busy as we head toward I-75, the early-morning commuters all racing toward their jobs and schools, but I ignore the world as I leave Miami. I'm worried about Liliana, what the hell her family has been up to, but then I wonder if she knows.

Has she been keeping secrets?

And I'm so lost in my thoughts that I almost miss Lionel's phone call when I'm an hour away. It rings and then cuts off before I pick up, only to ring again.

"I'm on my way. Be there in—"

"I won't be there, Micah," he says in a rush, and I hear yelling behind him. There's also what sounds like tires screeching. "Please take care of them. Don't let him harm them."

"Him? Rodolfo?" It cuts in and out, he's speaking but I can barely make out the words *hurt* and *guns* before the first shot is heard. "Lionel, where the fuck are you? What the hell is going on?"

"I've always approved of you and my sister. I know that she's safe with you and no one will treat her better." There's shouting, someone who sounds like Joaquin screaming to drive faster in Spanish. "Tell her we're so proud of her. Love them both."

He's saying goodbye, and my heart clenches. Sadness and anger overtake my senses, and the plastic in my hand groans. The tight grip on my phone cracks the area on both sides of the screen, and the last thing I want to do is lose connection if this shit breaks.

I press the speaker button then toss it aside, meeting Isaac's eyes through the rearview mirror.

"You'll tell them yourself." My voice is thick with emotions I can't bottle up. "Where are you? I'll come—"

"They have help, Micah. Intercepted us on our way to you and...*son of a bitch*!" he yells out, pure panic coming through his tone a second before there are more gunshots. Glass breaks on his end, then there's more yelling before I hear the unmistakable sound of an explosion ringing through the line.

A line that disconnects a second later, but his last plea rings through my ear...

Save them.

Chapter 14
LILIANA

omething's off.

I can sense it all around me.

It's this cloying and uncomfortable feeling and my skin itches, but outwardly, I remain calm.

No one is saying much, but the expression on many of the security personnel in Micah's building causes a shiver to run down my spine. Not the good kind, either. It's a choking matter—almost suffocating—but I don't know anyone here on enough of a personal level to feel comfortable asking.

Then, there's the fact Ligo is driving me again today as he did yesterday and the day before, but somehow, right now it's different.

Maybe I'm seeing things; like the tight set of his jaw and the white-knuckled grip he has on the steering wheel.

My car's been parked in the underground lot collecting dust while decisions are being made for me. Am I upset about it? Yes and no.

Had it been anyone else, I'd be kicking and screaming my way out of their plans, but not with Micah. This, for some reason, calms him. I don't want to stress him more than he's been the last few days.

My boss has been in and out of the office all week, staying only long enough to give me instructions on canceling anything and everything on his schedule or to handle it as I see fit. This isn't what I signed up for—my class project is weighing heavily on my mind—and I'm hitting a wall at every turn.

Yet every time I want to bring it up, I back down after taking one look at Micah. He's lost in his head.

Quiet. Contemplative. I can sense his anger brewing.

But why?

Then, there's the complete silence coming from my family. No one has called me or checked in, and while they can be at times tunnel-vision idiots, this is too much.

Not so much as a smoke signal to tell me all is okay, and my mind wanders. *Is it all connected? Are they hiding something from me?*

"They have no idea I moved," I mutter low, but if Ligo heard, he gives no indication. One minute I'm living in my mother's condo—an empty unit she uses whenever she's not traveling or in the Florida Keys with her friends—and then the next, I'm the newest tenant in a high-rise located on Brickell Avenue with over seventy floors and an ocean view.

"We're here, Ms." Ligo turns onto campus and then heads straight toward the main science building where my professor's office is located. How did he know? I have no clue, but maybe he went to school here. Or had family who did. "I'll wait for you close by."

"Thank you, but it's okay if you need to go. I can Uber it to the office after."

"No, ma'am. I'll be here."

"I don't know how long I'll be—"

"Take all the time you need."

"Okay." Exiting the SUV, I head inside the building, and Professor Duval's office door is toward the left not far from the entrance. It's ajar, but there are no voices coming from inside. Tentatively, I give a few soft knocks. "Professor?"

"Right behind you."

"Christ!" I squeak, whirling around to find my professor a few feet from me. In his late sixties and with a salt-and-pepper ponytail, he's carrying his backpack and a stack of books he can barely handle; I'm quick to reach forward and help. "I'll take these."

"Thank you, Ms. Armas." He moves past me but then pauses at his slightly open door. "I didn't leave this unlocked. What the hell?"

"Is something wrong, Professor?"

"I don't think." Pushing the door open, he walks inside and then looks around but finds nothing or no one and shrugs. "Please come inside. Have a seat."

"Okay." Not that he's paying much attention. Professor Duval puts everything away and then walks straight over to his mini fridge. From inside, he pulls out unsweetened iced tea, and I cringe, an expression he sees on my face. "What's wrong with this?"

"It should be illegal to drink it that way."

He snorts and pops the top before drinking half in one go. "It's not so bad."

"Not buying it."

"I don't either, but I tell myself this so I don't cave and my wife doesn't kill me."

"Now that makes sense." I'm still holding onto his books and place them down on the corner of his desk before sitting back. Professor Duval is behind his desk now, and this is the man I'm used to, stern face and a little impatient. "I'm sorry to bother you without a proper appointment. I know you're busy but—"

"What's going on?"

"I can't get a hold of Mr. Dunlap," I say, and going by his expression, he's not surprised by this. Is he no longer working with him? "I'm needing to log in my work study hours and discuss my final project."

Jeremy's left me with little to no choice in the matter. Since last week when he canceled on me, he's been pushing this back or just not answering my emails. Phone calls aren't being accepted either.

I'm being academically ghosted.

"That's because he quit."

"Come again?"

My outburst doesn't upset him; he merely waves it off. "Don't worry about the hours. I know you're responsible and we can always adjust it before the end of the semester. Matter of fact, do you have the company printout with your information?"

"I do."

"Then hand it over and I'll have the new teaching assistant handle it. She'll be starting next week...I think you know her. Ms. Samantha Cintek will be stepping in to help me for now."

"Doesn't she work for—"

"She's worked out a deal similar to Jeremy's. She has the right to divide her sixteen-hour work week as she pleases but must hold office hours on Fridays for students." Looking over at a letter on his desk, Mr. Duval reads through the subject, almost forgetting I'm here for a few minutes, but then looks up. "I'm actually surprised to see you, Liliana. How did you not know?"

My brows furrow. "Know what?"

"Jeremy quit because he sold his firewall hardware to Royce Cruise Lines and decided to—"

"What did you just say? Firewall hardware?" Oh, God. Please tell me I'm wrong in my assumptions. I'd shown him my work. He was interested, and thought it was good, but...

"You're brilliant, Lili," Jeremy speaks from beside me, his eyes on the screen as I show him my developments. So far, my program is in a software format, but could easily be adapted to hardware installed on company networks. It's meant to be for grand-scale work, not personal, and yet I can't get his approval to show my work as a final project. "How did you—"

"Then can I show it? Would Professor Duval be as impressed?"

"Please don't take offense to this, Liliana, but I'm trying to save you from yourself." Before I can ask him what that means, Jeremy is leaning back in his seat and rubbing a hand across his sparse facial hair. For a man in his late twenties, he looks a little tired. Always stressed and is fidgety, but everyone treats it like a quirk. He's of average build and average looks but has always been polite. He's a team leader now and is using his TA knowledge to lead our department alongside another man I've yet to meet. The latter started to work at Micah's company in February. "Duval likes his students to keep it simple. I can give you a list if you'd like—they're based on basic commands a graduate must excel at to find a job in this field."

"But I'm sure we can work around that. I'm implementing—"

"Do you trust me, Liliana? I've never lied to you." His question catches me off guard, simply because I don't know him outside of a working relationship. Sure, he's been helpful in the past when I've had questions and then appreciative when I gave him an unsolicited recommendation with Royce Cruise Line, but that's as far as it goes. "After graduation, you have one hell of a future ahead of you, but don't try to run before you can really walk. People like Duval don't like their toes to be stepped on."

To that, all I can do is nod and smile. It's a bit forced, but he doesn't notice. Jeremy is too preoccupied with my firewall work.

"I'm going to show you something, and I need your complete honesty, Professor." It's his turn to look confused, especially by my change in tone, but I take out my laptop and pull up the folder with my coding program. One by one, I show him the inception, my configurations—everything including the two emails Jeremy sent me asking questions.

One of which was my plans for availability after graduation.

"Fuck." One word from Duval, but it showed every bit of the anger I felt. "He stole from you!"

"Is this what you saw? Exact copy?"

"Yes. I'm sure of this." Rubbing a hand down his face, Professor Duval exhales roughly. "I need to report this, Ms. Armas. The school was going to award him a special recognition for his work while here, and now at Royce. This can't happen anymore. I'm under a moral obligation, if nothing else, to stop this."

"Understood." I'm defeated by this. Hurt. "Please do what you must. I'll return to the drawing board for my final project. Maybe Samantha can—"

"Why are you not making this the subject of your work? Liliana, this is brilliant work." Pointing at my laptop, he tilts his head in a silent question. My response is a nod, and he dives right in, reading through my notes, equations for the physical prototype, and then looks at me. "How soon can you have a model ready? How far along are you in the trial stages?"

"I've implemented the basics on a grand scale already, but I feel something is missing. It did what I wanted it to do, but—" I'm cut off by the ringing of my cell and frown. "My apologies. Please ignore it, I'll call whoever it is back."

Yet they call again. And again.

On the fourth call, Professor Duval waves toward my bag where the phone is. "Could be urgent."

"So it seems." Pulling the device from my bag, I press redial on a number I'm not familiar with, but the person who answers doesn't give me a chance to talk.

"Ms. Armas, I'm sorry to interrupt, but we need to go. They're waiting on us."

Chapter 15
LILIANA

P rofessor Duval is understanding as I rush to end our meeting, letting me go with a promise to keep him posted on my progress. He's impressed, it seems—offered to grade me based on what he's seen—but I'd rather show him the finished product.

Mentally, I've been going through the timeframe needed to complete my work and the materials I'll need to rush order for our presentation next month, but then I realize we're not heading to the office.

At the moment, Ligo is driving through Biscayne Boulevard, deviating from a route I know like the back of my hand while entering another one I'm familiar with. We pass the port, Bayside

Marketplace, and then bypass where I now live completely. Instead, he cuts through a few streets and backways to reach the 836 W, dodging traffic and bypassing the speed limit to then exit on Le June Rd a few miles later.

In no time, we're in the Hammocks Oaks & Lakes community and taking a left that leads us into an exclusive area where the wealthy citizens of Miami live who like to lead a more private life. They're close enough to enjoy amenities, but far away from the hustle and bustle of the city.

They want it that way. Have bought into that very style of life, and the area thrives with a mixture of old and new money.

Because you only get two types of wealthy people in a city like this: the flashy and the private.

They mix and socialize, but you can tell by location alone which kind of atmosphere you'll encounter, and the Royce family has always enjoyed the beauty in silence. The beach and Star Island are for those who want to be seen—have the public know you can afford the luxuries most people dream about, while those in exclusive areas like this one in Coral Gables have a different appreciation and level of extravagance.

The Royce family has a house here, and I'm right to suddenly feel wary when the gates open before we've stopped to announce our visit. Hell, I didn't even have to enter their house code into the reader that those with open access have—they've been expecting us.

And I'm proven right when Micah stands at the end of the drive, eyes bloodshot and reaching for my door before we've stopped. I'm unbuckled and yanked out within seconds, cradled against his warm body as he exhales roughly against the crown of my head. "I'll make this right, Rebel. I promise, baby."

I try to pull back, but he won't let me move. "Talk to me. Micah, what's going on?"

"Let's head inside."

"No. Tell me." I manage to choke out the words, my emotions and the events of the last few days beginning to weigh on me. Overwhelm me. It's frustration from not being able to crack who tried to implement a bug in his servers, my sudden move to one of his penthouses, and then Jeremy stealing my program and passing it off as his own—I'm fried. The last thing I need is to be hit with another surprise. "Please, Micah. I don't want to go in blind."

"It's best if we go inside, love. I'll be there with you every step." His voice is a bit hoarse; he needs me to not fight him on this, and I nod, letting him guide me inside. The first thing I'm met with is silence. Ominous and cold, and goosebumps break out on my skin as this feeling of dread overtakes me, but then we're inside his family's living room and my eyes flick from familiar face to familiar face until I notice two are missing.

His parents are here with sad expressions.

My mother and Beatrice are here with tears rolling down their cheeks.

Micah and his most trusted guards are here, anger coming off them in waves.

"Tell me I'm wrong, Micah." I'm begging. Praying to whatever God is listening to have this moment be nothing more than an emotional reaction and a mistake. Yet it doesn't happen. No one says anything, much less moves. No one but Micah, who wraps an arm around me and tucks me close.

His shuddered breaths—the way he's trying to control his own emotions further pull me into this nightmare, and for the first time since I've known him—I push him away.

"Lili, sweetheart, please come have a seat," Lester, Micah's father speaks, but it sounds off. My chest is heaving, my body shaking, and yet the two faces I want to see more than anything in this world are still missing.

Everyone but my father and brother are here, and suddenly I can't get air into my lungs. Can't stop the tears as they fall from my eyes, looking at all of them through blurry eyes as my world comes crashing down around me.

This pain is unlike anything I've ever felt before. Mom's the first one to break when our eyes meet, and the devastation on her face causes my legs to weaken and I slip, landing on both knees while another body shifts behind me. This time I don't fight him. Don't have anything left in me to give, but I do make out my low whisper and plea. "Tell me I'm wrong, Mom. Don't break my heart like this."

"I'm sorry, Mamita. Your father is gone." Mom's broken sob reverberates throughout the room, filling every single inch of space with her sorrow as Micah's mom, Helen, rushes to wrap her friend in a hug. Lester, for his part, places his hand on my mother's shoulder in a show of support—I don't want to see that.

All of this. Hear this.

It's a lie.

Has to be.

But then I hear her words again and again. Seven words, and they crushed my soul.

The world goes black around me.

"I won't stop until I find every person responsible, Rebel. They'll pay for this."

I don't know how long I've been asleep, but I come to slowly. Every part of my body aches. This infernal pain radiates from the center of my chest and out, striking across every limb and leaving me unable to move. It's why I hear his every word. Why I'm able to concentrate on his bourbon and citrus scent, using it to calm me long enough to lessen the knot in my throat and whisper his name.

It's low. Almost too low to hear, but his head snaps up from its place on my arm, and warm blue eyes meet my hazel ones. His smile is weak. Sad. "Hey, sweetheart."

"Hi." It comes out croaky, thick with my unleashed emotions as little by little everything hits me again. Except this time, I'm a little more prepared and bite back the sob fighting to break free. My bottom lip still wobbles, and seeing this, Micah's expression is one of raw pain. "Is there any water up here?"

"Of course. Give me a sec." He leaves me long enough to run to the theater room on this floor before rushing back. In his hand, he has water, Coke, and a bottle of iced coffee. Micah gives a shrug when I raise a brow. "Wasn't sure which one you'd want."

"I think the Coke for this one."

"How much do you remember, Lili?" That's how serious this is. He never calls me that. It's very rare that he does, and the times he has—each time it's because something is wrong.

"Enough to know I lost my father." Fuck, those words hurt to say. My throat feels as if pure acid had been poured down my esophagus and what's been left behind is torn, destroyed flesh. "Is that what happened? Where's Lionel?"

"Your brother's unconscious but alive. He'll be transferred later today from Orlando, but the attending there is just holding on until he wakes up. His injuries are minor."

A relieved breath whooshes out of me, but the relief doesn't last long. "How minor?"

"Can you sit up for me? Please?" I don't respond right away, but after a long minute, nod. "Thank you."

"How long have I been out?" I'm shifting, trying to pull myself up and against the headboard, but Micah slips in behind me. It surprises me at first, but then I'm thankful for the comfort. He tugs me between his parted legs, his broad chest against my back while a warm arm wraps around my waist. "Where's my father's—"

"Shhh, baby. I got you." His warmth seeps into my skin, but I'm cold. Crying and lost inside my grief because Micah didn't deny it. Instead, he confirms it a few agonizing minutes later when he whispers in my ear that they were ambushed in Orlando while on the way to meet him in Tampa.

How Lionel called him and he heard their car chase and then crash.

How this is tied to my father denying Rodolfo Diaz the land he wants for a touristy development. The man had sent people to intimi-date my father but caused a fatal crash instead. Lionel will be okay. His injuries are considered minor: four broken ribs, a hairline lacera-tion requiring stitches above his right eye, and he hasn't regained consciousness.

My poor brother. How will he react when he wakes up?

When he realizes that Dad is gone.

"They won't get away with this, Liliana." His lips are against my ear, exhaling roughly as his own emotions come through. He doesn't cry, but that doesn't lessen how much pain Micah's in. We all are. "Believe me, sweet girl. They'll pay with their blood."

And while I hear every word, I'm breaking apart in his arms all over again.

Cry and cry until I have nothing left, and then give in to my need for escape.

I fall asleep in his arms knowing when I wake again, I'll face this new reality once more.

DEVASTATION.

It's how I feel. All I can understand as I lie here in one of the Royce's guest bedrooms after falling asleep a little while ago. Not that I stayed down for long, but when Micah moved me and slipped out of the room to take a phone call, I feigned my slumber.

It's an odd sensation. Emotions that don't make any sense.

I know I need to face this. Be there for Mom, but all I keep thinking about is our last conversation. How I denied him my help with his next campaign because a part of me has always hated his political dreams.

Sure, we've had a great life materialistically speaking, but I've always wanted more from my parents. A more active role in my daily life, and now it all feels so stupid. I feel ungrateful for not appreci-ating the sacrifices made to give us a better life.

That Spanish-style mini-mansion he bought a little after winning his first term as Miami's mayor wasn't about showing off. It wasn't a victory trophy, but his attempt at normalcy—to give us a place that was just ours—even if we spent most of our time in the home provided for by the city. Those weekends spent grilling and swimming in the pool weren't about rubbing elbows with the wealthy, but about giving us memories.

Joaquin Armas wasn't making a point to his peers and constituents that he's a self-made man with the perfect accessories to tie the look together, but teaching his kids that a man that came from nothing could be something. From escaping tyranny in Cuba to a respected member of society, even if he wasn't always perfect.

I didn't see that. I didn't understand him.

It wasn't all about money, greed, or power.

For so long, I thought what mattered most to him was having the gorgeous wife and two smart, well-connected children within our social circle. How good our academic achievements and sports trophies made him look, but in reality, he loved us in his own way.

"I'm sorry, Dad."

"He could never be angry at you, Lili. You were the apple of that man's eye," Mom says, her voice a nearly broken whisper, and my head snaps in her direction. She's standing by the doorway, face splotchy and body shaking, and I'm scrambling toward her on my next breath. "Oh, Lili…baby, tell me this isn't real."

"I love you, Mom." That's all I can tell her. Lying won't bring him back. Noting will, and I hug her tight, following her down to the ground as we cry. Her pain is mine. Our tears can't be stopped.

For my father.

For her husband.

For Lionel, who's not here, and we can only pray he's truly okay and this nightmare doesn't land another blow. Because our lives will never be the same again. Nothing ever will be.

Chapter 16
MICAH

W atching her cry over her brother's ICU bed is heartbreaking.

It took a few days, but he's been transferred to a hospital in Coral Gables and is under the constant care of an old family friend to both the Armas and Royce families. He's the chief physician there and has assured us he'll receive the best care, but it's an endless waiting game and I'm not sure how much more Rebel can take.

Her sobs haunt me. The way she threw herself on his bed and begged him to wake up is something I will never forget, and while her pain is the cause, my wrath is the effect.

I've been patient.

Waiting and holding back so I can take care of her, but no more.

Rodolfo Diaz is a dead man walking. He has until after the funeral before I strike.

Chapter 17
MICAH

It's been a week now since her father's death, and Lionel hasn't woken up. We're told it's just his body giving itself the time it needs to recuperate, but we can no longer wait to bury Joaquin. The decision is out of my hands, no matter how much I'd like to make this all go away for my rebel. There's nothing anyone can do as we stand in front of his closed casket, something his wife insisted on—she can't face seeing him like this—as loved ones and friends gently toss sunflowers atop it before it's buried. One by one, his closest come to pay their respects before turning and giving their condolences to both Celia and my Liliana.

Neither of the two manages to utter more than a tear-filled thank you, but everyone understands, and I do what I can to take care of them both. Her grief guts me, but I know one day it will all be okay.

With time, she'll get past this too.

The lies. The hurt. The truth.

"Don't leave me, Micah." Rebel's words are low and her voice is raw. Those beautiful eyes that I love so much are red-rimmed, and her sadness reaches out to me, lashing at the heart inside my chest that beats only for her. Everything I do is for her. "Need you."

Yet nothing destroys a man more than to watch the woman he loves suffering. Her pain is mine, and it's so deeply rooted into my marrow that I physically ache—my chest constricts at the sight of her tear tracks and splotchy skin, the sleep deprivation no amount of makeup can hide.

She's questioning the mortality of everyone around her.

She's lost herself in this deep cycle of anguish.

I worry about her and how she'll deal with the anger that will follow.

I'll happily hunt and then force our enemies to kneel while presenting her the honor of the kill. She can slit their throat while I sit back and call her my perfect, good girl.

"I'll always be here, Liliana. For the rest of our lives."

REBEL'S finally sleeping after a rough afternoon, body wrapped in soft blankets while I lay beside her on the bed. We're back at my building, the penthouse she now calls home because she refused to go anywhere but where I am, and our families understood. Celia's with my parents and will visit her son later tonight, but she also needed some rest.

Rest we encouraged via a sleeping pill our family doctor prescribed.

"I've got you, sweetheart. I'll kill them all in your name."

As if she hears me, her bottom lip trembles and a shudder wracks her sinuous frame. Just like it did the moment reality set in and grief hit—each sharp lash dealt by fate struck her small frame until she could hardly stand. Her sobs—each second she's in pain—is a direct insult to me.

I've had to watch her break down and be sedated twice now.

Those two instances are going to cost Diaz and his son heavily. More than they're willing to pay.

Another jerky movement shifts her, bringing her closer to me, and her soft breaths fan across my chest. I'm turned toward her while counting the discreet blinking red light in her ceiling vent that shows the camera there is recording. It's not the only one in here either, and I wonder what she'll think the day I show her where each device is located.

Yet right now, I can't think past her distress. It cuts me and eviscerates the last thread of humanity I cling to where she's concerned because when it comes to her, there will never be a second or inch of space between us. Not now or the day I claim what's mine—give her my last name.

I know where she is at all times. Anything less than her happiness is unacceptable.

Moreover, the proof is in the cameras embedded inside each wall she inhabits.

In the alarm clock on her nightstand to the right.

In the A/C vent above my little rebel's bed, and inside her closet via a hidden passageway.

In the frame of a painting across from her four-poster bed, one she loves of a large black and white piece I commissioned from a popular tattoo artist of the work he did on my sleeve last year. It's a bit gloomy. Haunting, yet beautiful. An attraction to the darkness and unpredictable nature of the ocean I share with the beauty sleeping now against my chest, sighing as I pull her closer.

Because Liliana Armas is no wallflower.

Not shy or timid, something I adore about her and find little ways to nurture.

I'll make this right, sweet girl. One day, everything will be okay.

I'll make it so. Take every blow and kill in her name while she finds peace in my bed each night.

In her sleep, her face pinches tight—as if reacting to the ire vibrating beneath my skin—and I force myself to calm down. I keep my touch light on her back, gentle sweeps up and down the length of her spine while matching my breathing to hers, a rhythmic cadence that I follow while the soft light of a nearby salt lamp casts a gentle glow across her delicate features. Her face is still flushed and pink—the track marks left behind by her earlier tears are evident in the streaks of mascara dried down each perfect, rosy cheek.

She never removed her makeup, and I fix that by reaching carefully behind me and opening her bedside drawer. In here she has a bunch of things that don't make sense to me—products that I wouldn't know what to do with—but the small packet of wipes at the top is all I need.

It takes some maneuvering, but I manage to take a single sheet out before tossing the rest aside. I'm gentle as I wipe each cheek and under her eyes, removing every smudge until what's left is her soft face with just a hint of splotchiness left behind from days of crying.

And while the decisions I make won't always be the ones she approves of, I do it with love.

Because the day she walks down the aisle to me, everything will be as it should always have been.

AN HOUR LATER, I slip from her bedroom and back to my penthouse to grab a quick shower. It's been a long day and it isn't done for me yet, but I left a small note on her bedside table letting her know where I am on the off chance she wakes up.

The sedation medication was meant for them to get the rest both mother and daughter needed—more than the meager three or four hours a night my rebel had been surviving on since this nightmare for her began.

Grief is a horrible thing; I know that.

It hurts and leaves you gasping while the hole in your chest makes it hard to breathe.

I'd experienced that same feeling of loss when my grandfather died, and I still remember how she never left my side. We were teens then and had only known each other for less than a year, but she fought everyone to stay with me when I needed her the most. Helped me the same way I'll take care of her now.

I'll love her through this. Be there in whatever capacity she needs me.

Entering my living room, I find a visitor and I'm not surprised. "I see you've made yourself at home?"

"It's what parents do after their kids have their own place. We return the favor."

I snort. "What's that supposed to mean?"

"Means I can come and go as I please while using everything in your house. That I'll touch and use and leave a mess behind for you to clean."

A small smile tugs at my lips; he's being ridiculous. More so because the man is anal about the cleaning and organization of the home, more than Mom has ever been. "Is that what this is? A payback visit?"

"You can call it something like that."

"I call bullshit." Walking over to the bar cabinet in the corner by the fireplace—a feature that makes no sense in a city like Miami but I added it because Liliana loves the look—I open the door and pick up a bottle of whiskey. No glass. This occasion doesn't call for one. Instead, I flick the top away and then take the seat across from him and take a deep pull. "Or is this because you have some information I need?"

"Rodolfo called me."

"What did the dead son of a bitch want?"

"Same as before, but now with an in." At that, I raise a brow. Take another drink as my mind runs through possibilities, and there are only two possible scenarios where it could work for him.

The governor agrees without red tape or investigations for a fee.

The deputy mayor was coerced into pushing his agenda for a donation.

Both involve money, just in different ways: personal gain or political push.

"And?"

"Joseph Wilburn."

"Already? He's barely had time to warm the chair, and he's already making this kind of a political stance?"

"He's always been in Diaz's pocket. That was Rodolfo's ace in the hole."

"Did you know?" I spit this out through clenching teeth, my jaw ticking. I'd never forgive him if he did. "Did you hide this from me?"

"Do not insult me, Micah." Dad swirls the amber liquid in his glass, his eyes on mine before taking a sip. A drink he'd been nursing since before I walked in. "I want that motherfucker's head more than you do. He betrayed the trust I put in our working partnership, tried to use my family, and hurt my friends in the name of a few extra zeros in a portfolio that didn't need it. Those tears my future daughter-in-law has cried are unforgivable, and I want his blood. That of everyone involved."

"Are you sure you're ready to dirty your hands like that?"

"He wouldn't be my first or last, son."

"Good."

Because my first strike is past due.

Chapter 18
LILIANA

"How are you, sweetie?" Luna asks from across the booth, giving one of my hands a gentle squeeze. She invited me out to lunch today, and even though no part of me wants to be here—anywhere at the moment—I couldn't refuse her. Not just because her husband is a mafia kingpin, but because he's family.

Distant, though. I've maybe met him and his brother, Ivan, three times, but we have the same blood, nonetheless. And this is what relatives do in moments like these; we might not be close in our day to day, but they show up in moments of need.

It's why I crawled out of bed after spending the last few days after Dad's burial avoiding reality. Why I showered and changed and I'm giving her small smile as I squeeze her fingers back, saying what I can't with words because of the sudden knot in my throat.

Swallowing hard, I give myself a minute to gather my emotions. Something she doesn't rush, either. If anything, the soft look on her face tells me she understands and is patient.

"To be honest, I have no idea how to feel." It's the truth. "Everything is so messed up, and I feel lost. Angry and lost."

"And you're allowed to, Mami. Nothing can prepare you for moments like these." Our waiter chooses to approach our table then, and I'm so thankful that she orders for us. Nothing big. Just a frita; a Cuban-style burger and some fries with a pineapple soda for each. And for the first time in days, my stomach truly rumbles.

I've been eating to appease Micah and my mother, the latter of whom I haven't seen since Monday, and it's Thursday now.

"Have you eaten here before?" she asks, and I catch her eyes looking behind her. The booth-style seating makes it hard, neither of us being gifted in the height department, but I catch the twitch of her lips. "Thiago's mom is behind all the recipes. She's an amazing cook."

"No. I haven't." For some reason, that hits me. *Family is family, no matter what side of the law they sit on.* "But I'm glad you're giving me the chance to."

"And why wouldn't she?" a voice says from behind me, causing her to laugh. "It's not my fault your attention was set in the wrong direction. I'm unpredictable if nothing else, my wife."

"You're here, bebe. That's not something shocking."

"Says you. I came in through the other door." His deep timbre fills every square inch of this cute restaurant, and a few people look over with amused expressions while Luna giggles. My guess is this scenario isn't surprising to them, his openness and affection, but what does shock me is the slight resemblance to my father, when Dad was younger. It's like looking at an old and worn picture from when we were kids, if my Joaquin Armas was a beefed-up body-building mafia don.

It both hurts and soothes me to see a man that for all intents and purposes, I do not know.

The large man walks past me and slips into our booth beside his wife. It's a tight fit, she's almost squished between him and the wall, but Luna doesn't seem to mind in the least. If anything, her blush tells me she loves his attention. That he shows up unannounced, and often.

As they settle next to each other, his eyes meet mine and all I feel is familiarity. My lips twitch. "Thiago De Leon, I presume."

"Hello, little cousin." His large frame leans over and somehow manages to lay a tiny kiss on my forehead, and the moment feels important. "It's nice to finally meet you, although I wish it was under better circumstances."

"Me too." Behind me, there's a sudden noise, a little crash as if someone dropped a plate, but when I turn to look, I find nothing. Yet I know I'm not crazy. And the way Thiago watches the area is full of satisfaction, maybe a little bit of approval. "Did you guys hear that?"

"Hear what?" he asks, amusement dripping from the two words.

"Like something broke or someone tripped..." *Am I hearing things?*

"You know, I've spent a lifetime hearing those same little *sounds* you just did," Luna says, a smirk on her face. There's also the way her brow arches, but I'm not catching on. "Mine isn't as subtle as yours seems to be, though. He's kind of a brute. Not so—"

"I don't have a boyfriend." My heart accelerates a bit, but it's just the wishful desire that Micah would ever see me that way. I won't deny that he's been amazing these last few weeks. Always near. Taking care of me in any way I'll let him, and it's created a little blossoming kernel of hope in me.

One I need to squash. Another heartbreak right now will end me.

"You sure about that?" Thiago nods at something behind me, his expression much more serious than it's been up until then. There's this edge of danger in him, something dark, and surprisingly, I'm not afraid of it. More like intrigued. "Because I think you're not seeing the bigger picture. Not realizing that nothing is ever as it seems, and that the solution to everything is much closer than you think."

"That's pretty ominous, yet it's like you said nothing at all."

Thiago laughs loudly at that, head thrown back. "You're a smart ass, Liliana. I like that."

"So I've been told." I can't help myself. Nor do I stop the genuine quirk of my lips. Our food is delivered then, and it's a lot. The burger is loaded with all the fixings, not to mention the almost obscene amount of shoestring fries it comes with. "How am I supposed to finish this?"

"With your mouth."

"Funny, Luna," I say, popping two fries into my mouth. Salty and fried perfection.

"What can I say—I'm hilarious." Taking a bite from her frita, she hums in satisfaction before reaching over and pulling a piece of paper from her bag after wiping her hands. It's a printout of some sort, but I can't see what's on the white sheet with the way she's folded it. Luna pushes it across the table next to my right hand. "There's a traitor in the Royce company, Liliana. He's been paid a lot of money—made promises by the same people responsible for the accident involving your father and brother. Be careful, honey. This isn't over."

Pushing my plate aside, I open the report and find multiple trans-actions of over one hundred thousand dollars at a time. I'm counting, and there are eight of them in total. They're also to the same person, and the originating account details are city-provided.

The first six numbers are unique and the same for every Dade County employee. No other banking institution is allowed to use this identifying sequence.

"How did you get this information?" It comes out harsher than I intend, but neither is put off by the edge in my tone. "This is a lot of money being paid off to the owner of this account."

She shrugs and takes another big bite. "I worked in the forensics department for MDP for years, Liliana. So did my uncle and cousin before their early retirements, and we've kept in touch with the friends we made over the years. They're always happy to keep us aware of anything catching the interest of the department, and there's a detective looking into these fraudulent expenses."

"So tread carefully either way?" I hedge, lips pursing as I'm reading the list again.

"You won't get caught." Thiago pushes my plate in front of me and I look up, catching his not-so-subtle demand that I eat. "I'm sure you can hack into the system and cover your tracks, or are you not as good as some people claim?"

"I'm better."

"That's what he said." Before I can ask him what he means, my cousin points at the food. "Eat, Liliana. You have a lot of people worried about you."

"What about…" I trail off as another waitress brings over a large plate of rice, beans, and picadillo with fried sweet plantains. "Never mind."

No one says anything else, and after a few minutes, I give in and eat. More than I thought I would. All of it. I devour the entire burger and half my fries before looking up, and finding the two of them watching me with matching satisfied expressions.

"Good?"

"I'll be back again, Thiago."

"Glad to hear it, and anytime. You're family."

"Thank you." Giving the clock on the wall a quick glance, I catch the time and grimace. "I better get going, though. Promised my boss I'd stop by the—" The sound of my cell phone ringing cuts me off. At first, I thought it'd be Micah to verify when I'd be stopping by, but it's not. It's the hospital. "Hello."

"Hi, I'm looking for a Liliana Armas?"

"She's speaking."

"Good. Because your brother's awake and asking to see you."

To say I'm nervous on my way to the hospital would be putting it mildly. My entire body is jittery—excited—but there's an edge of worry too. Not just for what Luna and Thiago showed me, but his parting words.

Don't close yourself off from seeing the bigger picture, little cousin. Men oftentimes aren't the best at expressing their emotions, but their actions fill that void. A man who loves you will move mountains for you—eliminate any obstacle in your way—before you're even aware of the dangerous terrain up ahead. They'll take care of the little things, and make sure you're never without, and by the time you're ready to walk the path, the stones are smooth and flat and without the possibility of inflicting pain.

I can see that in him. How he nurtures his wife, but he's wrong about one thing…

There's no one in my life willing to sacrifice and give for me. Not in a romantic way.

Surprisingly, traffic isn't too bad and I make it to the hospital quicker than I thought. Parking is a little different, nothing near the entrance for three floors, but my luck changes on the next one. It's right beside the elevators and I slide in, taking it before someone else does.

Because of his injuries, he's been in the ICU for the last ten days. It was the maximum occupancy for a patient unless the case has extenuating circumstances. The mild swelling in his brain has gone down, something the doctors found after the first twenty-four hours. At first, they put it down to the hair-line laceration and him being concussed, but when the CT scan came back, his diagnosis changed from mere laceration to fracture.

We've visited him, mom and I, but for some reason not together.

She hasn't been around as much as I expected after everything that's happened, but I guess that's her way of grieving and I'm no one to judge. However, I won't deny that I'm highly disappointed when I walk into the unit and don't find her there.

"Liliana, so good to see you!" Karrie, the nurse in charge of his care, exclaims when she sees me. She's a mid-fifties woman with the looks of someone who's thirty-something and glowing. Lively. Always has an amazing attitude. "We were working on his admittance into a general ward this morning when he started groaning. It was low at first, but over the last few hours Lionel's become more alert—responsive to stimuli—and now he's asking for you."

"Jesus," I breathe out as tears gather at the corner of my eyes, so much tension draining from my body. "You have no idea how happy I am to hear this."

"That's what Mr. Royce said."

"Mr. Royce? Micah Royce?"

"Yes." Kerrie smiles at me. "He's the one who pointed out the changes in Lionel's behavior." She pauses for a second and leans over as if she's telling me a secret. "Mr. Royce comes every day before visiting hours, but the head physician approved of this so no one questions it."

"I didn't know."

"Seems he's a private man." Over the intercom speakers, a code is read and she rushes off without another word, leaving me a few doors down from my brother's room. Won't deny I'm a little nervous about seeing him. The things I need to tell him won't be easy, but I still knock on his door wearing a false sense of bravado and a smile.

"Come in."

Peeking my head in, I'm happy to see him at ease. Completely awake. "Hi."

"Come in, little sis." His complexion is a little pallid, but the bruising that formed above his eye after the accident is now a fading greenish yellow. His staples are also out, the line left behind still a bit red, but that'll heal with time and the damage left behind will be minimal. "Sit with me."

"Can I get a hug first?" I hate how my voice shakes when I ask, but so many emotions are battering me at once—nervousness being the predominant one. *How do I tell him?*

"I'd be pissed if you didn't." Those words and the soft way he says them break the dam and I'm rushing to his side, hugging him while being mindful of his injuries. His shaky hand goes to the back of my head and he holds me, lets me cry and make a mess, but my big brother doesn't care. Occasionally, I get a low *shushing* sound in comfort. "It's going to be okay, Lili. We'll get through this."

That catches me by surprise and I pull back, careful not to jostle his ribs. "You know?"

"Everything. More than you do."

"What does that mean, Lionel?" My voice cracks and tears still fall from my eyes, but I don't wipe them away. Instead, I'm focusing on that phrase. How three different people have said the same thing in such a short span of time. What am I missing here? *It'll be okay. It'll be okay.* How the hell will any of this ever be okay? "Explain yourself, because I cannot handle any more surprises. I'm a mess."

"I can't explain it *yet*, but I do need a favor in the meantime."

"A favor? Are you kidding me?" An incredulous huff leaves me and so does the fight—I take the seat beside his bed while he grips my hand. "Unless it's about food, water, or to pick up Beatrice to come take care of you…"

"You'd say no to me after just waking up?" Lionel's trying to soften me up by teasing, but I'm not buying it. None of it. *How long was he actually awake before they called me?* He's too refreshed, and there's not a single hint of drowsiness in him. "That's not very nice of you."

"I'm never nice according to you." My eyes narrow at him. "Now, are you going to continue hiding things from me?" Instead of answering my question, he points toward a manila envelope I hadn't paid attention to sitting atop a rolling table against the opposite wall.

It's nondescript. No real reason to draw the eye in a situation like this, but now that I've seen it, it's like a beacon. "What's that?"

"I'm assuming you've already seen Thiago and Luna?"

My head snaps back to him. *Something is definitely wrong here.* "How the hell do you know that?"

"Because I need your help, Lili. So does Micah."

At that moment, my best friend walks in the door holding a takeout bag from a nearby restaurant and pauses; I arch a brow. She doesn't say anything at first, blushing a bit, and I'm almost amused by how she squares her shoulders and then throws me a soft smile.

"Hey, you," Beatrice says, walking over to give me a quick kiss on the cheek before pulling back. "You hungry? I brought plenty."

"I can see that." And I do, the carry-out brown bag is full. It's more than enough to feed a group of six. "But I'm wondering how you got here so fast? Did my brother call you before me?"

Lionel clears his throat; his expression tells me to leave it.

Beatrice shifts her eyes to his, hoping he says something to save her.

And I'm freaking pissed at him when her eyes dim at his silence.

"Oh, I was already here when he woke up. Got the all clear from his doctor, too." Beatrice shifts, and I give her a nod and smile even though this further cements my brother's been awake longer than Karrie explained. *Why lie, though?* But I play along for now, sooner or later she'll tell me the truth. "I sent your mom home to get some rest...I didn't mind staying to help."

"Thank you for that, babes. We all appreciate you so much." *And If my brother weren't injured and waking up from a coma, I'd punch the jerk face for you.* Standing, I walk over and hug her while smiling at Lionel from over her shoulder. Going to mess with him a little, too. "But you should get some rest, Bea. I know school's hectic right now."

"I'm fine. I swear—"

"Why don't we leave this here with him, and go catch up for a bit."

"No," they say in unison, and I bite back a laugh. *Why can't they quit this weird flirting and admit they like each other? It'd make everything so much easier.*

"Okay. You guys have fun, then." And while she begins taking out his food and serving Lionel, I pick up the envelope and place it inside my purse. I get the feeling I'm not going to like what I find inside.

Chapter 19

MICAH

PRESENT...

I'll be there in twenty. Handle the parcel with care.
~Royce

It's been twenty minutes since that text came in, and I'm on my way to the docks where I keep Esmeralda. Isaac is already there and waiting, keeping watch over three people who have a lot of explaining to do.

I want to hear the excuses.

I'll wait for the tears.

And then I'll create a human sacrifice in her honor because she is my goddess.

Pulling into the company's private port, I find the gates already open and drive straight through, only rolling my window down long

ONE RULE

enough to send a quick wave to the night guard on duty. He's been
with my family for years, understands discretion, and immediately
rushes to close the electric metal doors right behind me.

The next thing I notice is how dark it is. Not a single lamp post is
on, and the only source of light is coming from right above the
hangar's door. That's it. The building itself has blacked-out-
windows; you can't see inside, and it sits close to the area where
cruise ships are dry-docked and worked on, housing at times the
materials used and mechanical parts needed for repairs.

Today, though, it's nearly empty. Esmeralda is three-quarters of
the way complete, and while the interiors of a project of this magni-
tude consume a lot of space, my contractor has a creative solution.
Where this place can house a few large vessels at once, one of the
occupants at the moment is a container ship with everything needed
to refurbish Esmeralda and a crane to make moving each pallet easy.

It's changed the speed in which the tradesmen can move. Having
things accessible from different ports of entry helps depending on
what floor you're on.

A shout in the distance comes through clearly, the sounds from
the Port of Miami now filling the night. Lost in my thoughts, I'd
somehow muffled the screech of moving containers and the clang
from unloading shipments. Then, there's screaming out of orders and
the heavy machinery—how it all creates a havoc-filled symphony for
my guests to enjoy.

Something that makes the way I forced the doors to open—how
they slam into the walls behind them—reverberate throughout the
large warehouse a bit chilling. So close to help, but they won't be
heard.

No one to hear your cries for help.

Three heads snap in my direction, each with a varying expression
of the same emotion. Doesn't deviate from that shared feeling that's
causing their airways to constrict for a moment as if someone is
wrapping their hands around their throats.

Fear. Unadulterated fear.

ELENA M. REYES

It's in the way their eyes widen and bodies start to shake within the limits of their binds, each body strapped to a metal post by their arms. How they sweat inside a well-air-conditioned room, the open space well-lit and smelling clean. Like Pinesol, but beneath it there's a touch of piss that makes me look down, and I find the man to the right standing barefoot in a puddle of his own making.

"Isaac."

"Good evening, boss." He's never been one for a lot of words, but I see amusement on his face.

"Interesting night?"

"You can say that." Isaac relaxes in his seat while I take the one across from him, a little table between us. He's been playing solitaire, his last card facing up but not placed yet. "They have some incredibly entertaining stories to tell. So much rich bullshit."

"I'd like to hear some of these *stories*." There are two Teflon coolers within arm's reach, and I pop their lids: one is filled with beers and ice, and the other with acid. "Drink?"

"No. I'm good."

Nodding, I pull out a dark lager and using my key, I remove the cap. It's a trick Lionel's dad taught us the year we turned twenty-one. He got a kick out of how hard we struggled to make it work.

I broke five keys during that time.

Lionel nearly cracked his tooth fighting to pry one stubborn top off.

"Who wants to start?" No one makes a sound, so I help them. In one deep pull, I drink down half the contents and then smash the bottle into the head of the man who got closest to my rebel.

He's the youngest of the three here tonight at only twenty-five. No wife. No girlfriend. No kids.

However, the saddest part is the way he's already crying. Tears run down his face, mixing with the blood flowing from the cut just given. It's creating a mess on his dirty white shirt, and I'm disgusted by the sight.

Pussy.

152

"I'd start talking if I were you, Mr. Ricardo Vega." His eyes widen, as do those of his partner in crime. Because if I know who one is, I'm also aware the man beside him is his older cousin and a royal fuckup. They're gophers for our newly appointed mayor, the same idiot who decided a little padding of his pockets and the promise of political backing is worth the life of a man who helped him run for the position of deputy mayor last election.

He could've moved up in the ranks after Joaquin won his second run.

He could've built connections and made a name for himself while serving as a backup.

"We can come to an agreement, Micah." Joseph chooses that moment to speak, but I pay him no mind, my eyes remaining on the younger Vega. Ricardo's looking anywhere but at me, his body shaking as the pain and his fear of what's to come mix. "You're a businessman, Royce. We'll pay you anything you want for you to forget this indiscretion. Surely, the little whore isn't worth that—"

My chair's thrown back and the table almost topples over as my fist connects with Joseph's mouth, causing his head to snap back against the metal post. It clangs and his eyes roll back from the force, teeth chipping off in bits with each new blow I land. He's going to hurt for what he just said, and I'll start by destroying his perfectly fake image.

More and more pieces break, tearing at my skin while I unleash all the pent-up ire that's been brewing. I don't stop when his top lip splits, the cut getting larger with every punch that follows. I'm going to make sure he's unrecognizable when I transport him out of the country and into international waters.

Turning my arm, my elbow meets his nose, and the satisfying crunch of bone fills the space. To me, it's a beautiful sound, while Ricardo vomits and his cousin, Amado, closes his eyes. They've gone pallid now. Whimpering.

Where are the tough men who followed Liliana yesterday? Where's that bravado?

"Start talking, Ricardo. Don't make me ask you again." Turning my back to them, I tap a semi-conscious Joseph on the cheek. His head lolls a bit, but he's aware enough for what I'm about to do to him. Ricardo begins to speak, but I can't understand anything past the mumbles and hyperventilating tears. "I'm going to give you five minutes to gather yourself. Understood?"

"Yes." Again with the low meekness.

"Isaac, start a timer and then come give me a hand."

It takes him but a second and then he's right beside me. "It's going."

"Good. Then help me take him for a short walk." The rope around his wrists is tight, cutting into Joseph's circulation, and I have to use a knife to get him loose. Isaac's set out a few things for me while I help Joseph understand the error of his ways, but none of these items are working for me.

Instead, I want something that sends a message. A gun, knife, and sledgehammer aren't enough.

So while I hold up Miami's interim mayor and Isaac walks ahead of me to the coolers, my eyes shift around the room. While he removes the cooler with our drinks and then opens the lid of the one with the acid, I find a fishing line and hook.

A few of the men who've worked on Esmeralda have fished here after work or on the weekends—with my permission on a day off. Toward the end and on the left of this port there's a pier that leads a bit out into the water, used before by my father when he'd pull up on one of his fishing boats. It's not too high that you're not able to hop on and walk onto the property, but in deep enough water that a smaller vessel can ease in and out without a problem.

It's why there's always fishing equipment. Sometimes people leave it or forget.

The strong smell of the acid hits my senses then and my nose twitches, as does that of everyone else inside the warehouse, but I don't give Joseph time to realize what I'm about to do. He's moaning and mumbling pitiful cries, his mouth destroyed from my punches while bloody fragments of teeth are embedded into his skin.

Yet that's the least of his troubles because a second later, I've put on my protective gloves and force his hands inside the container to just a little above his wrists. His reaction is instant and he thrashes, tries to knock me off and take his hands out, but the click of a gun and the feel of the muzzle against his temple makes him pause. He's going into shock, but I don't allow him to remove his hands while a faint buzzing sound greets my ears.

Turning my head, I give a nod to Isaac who removes the gun and steps back enough that I can make eye contact with Ricardo. "Start talking."

"He offered us twenty thousand a piece and a house if we removed a few obstacles in his way."

"Keep going," I say, but I'm calculating how long his hands have been under now. At the very least three minutes. "What were the obstacles?"

"Joaquin Armas and Liliana Armas." At the mention of her name, my lip curls over my teeth but I don't say anything. I'm biting back my ire as he continues to talk, explaining how Mr. Wilburn gave the go-ahead to do whatever they wanted to the Armas family, and that meant putting their hands on Liliana. "He made a promise to his nephew that includes her somehow. That she's in the way, and we were to scare her into signing over some work and then disappear."

"Disappear how?" I grit out, and from the corner of my eyes, I catch Amado shaking his head. He's a problem easy to fix, and I release my hold on Joseph long enough for Isaac to step in. He's not to be removed until he passes out; I'm keeping him alive as a gift for my in-laws.

Lionel is owed his pound of flesh. All of them are.

Within seconds, I have the gloves off and I'm reaching for the gun in Isaac's back pocket, pulling it out and firing a single shot. It's a clean one, too. Straight in and out, but the spray of blood and matter reaches Ricardo, who now wears a horrified expression.

Amado hangs there limply without ever having a said a word in his defense, but I'd already read his information and he was scared, not remorseful. Given the opportunity to do it again, he would without a second thought.

He's killed before, something Ricardo hasn't done, and because of his stupidity and desire for easy money, I'll make sure he never sees the next sunrise.

"I won't ask again. Disappear how?"

"Please don't kill me." He's fighting against his bindings, gagging between his cries for help. No one can hear him. No one will save him. "Let me run away. I won't tell anyone what you did to us."

"That's not what I asked, Mr. Vega. Answer the question."

"I can't. Please, let me go."

"I never quite understood why people like to make things difficult for themselves," Isaac interjects, laying a passed-out Joseph on the ground. His hands are destroyed—yet he still has full function—but the skin's completely melted off and the acid has begun to eat some of the tissue and muscle beneath.

It looks very painful.

"Agreed." My next shot also hits its mark and embeds itself in his left toe. It takes the big one clean off, his foot bouncing up from the impact. "What were you going to do to her?" His scream rends the air. His body tries to bend into itself from the pain, but I'm not moved. I'm furious. "Speak up, or I'm going to empty this entire clip in you. I'll pick my shots. Make sure to avoid any major arteries and make the bleed out a slow one. Is that understood?"

"Y-Yes." A sob.

"Then answer the simple fucking question."

"W-We could do anything we'd like to h-her, but ultimately she needed to die."

"And that was your biggest mistake. She's always had me to protect her." The last bullet to dislodge today mimics the wound left on Amado's forehead. Like his cousin, the kill shot ends Ricardo's short life while I calmly walk over to the fishing equipment and pick up what I need before donning a new pair of gloves. Latex this time.

It was only ever going to end this way.

Thiago also knew this much when he watched me stand behind them inside of his family's restaurant and then knock them unconscious with a single blow to the head from the butt of this same gun. Ligo had been quick to spot them following her earlier in the day and he let me know immediately, earning himself a nice bonus from me.

They'd been cocky and so full of themselves to walk into a mafia family's place of business and not expect consequences, especially when there's a familial tie between the De Leons and the victim.

Not that De Leon had to lift a finger, because she's mine.

To protect. To love. To claim.

Threading the hook with the line, I begin to sew their mouths then eyes shut. It's a simple catch-stitch. The pattern is easy enough, and while the cleaning crew begins to rid the scene of the mess we created, Isaac helps me remove the bodies.

They have separate destinations for now. One will be held as a prisoner until the time's right, and the other two will deliver a clear message to Rodolfo and his son.

You don't look or touch at what's mine.

Chapter 20
LILIANA

I can't stop thinking about the information Lionel and Thiago gave me.

It's been days now of me going over it in my head. Trying to make a rational decision, but all I've done is spend days and nights staring at my computer screen until finally giving in to my exhaustion around six a.m. each day. Four of them, to be exact.

To go or not to go. That is my conundrum.

My initial reaction was to get home and start accessing Dad's files, see if there's anything on the financials for his subordinates to go on, and start digging without me having to hack a government office, but then I sat back and just stared at the screen. To access his files, I'd need to go to his house, and I'm just not ready to do that.

Even when they moved him out of the mayoral estate so Joseph Wilburn could settle in, I didn't go. Couldn't.

Instead, I let Micah and my mother handle it, and she herself seemed different after. Mom's been nervous and antsy for a while now. It's actually getting worse. She's mentioned wanting to get away a few times now but hasn't because at the time Lionel had not regained consciousness, yet now that he has, there's nothing really stopping her. Not really.

I need to get away, Mamita. My heart isn't here, and I need to mend it. Make myself whole again, and one day soon you'll understand why.

She said that to me more than a week ago, tears in her eyes, and although I want to be mad at her for leaving again at a time like this, a part of me understands. He was my father, but that was her soulmate—and they never stopped loving each other.

Their divorce never quite made sense to me or anyone close to the family, but they went through with it, never once being angry. No mudslinging. No outrageous demands. The entire ordeal was the most amicable thing I've ever seen—no bitterness, but full of hope—and it hurt them equally.

Mom wanted him to be around more, travel and enjoy their empty-nesters stage in life.

Dad wanted to push his political career as far as he could without holding back.

There wasn't a mistress or any hatred, just two adults who drifted apart yet still adored each other. And it was because of that love that Celia Armas stepped aside so Joaquin Armas could fulfill his dreams without her holding him back, something my father was always aware of.

He never stopped trying to coax her back home.

She enjoyed those moments when his attention was solely focused on her.

But where did that leave me now? Sure, I could ask for her help —his passcode to everything has always been a combination between all three of our birthdays, and it's usually in the order we were born in, from oldest to youngest—but involving her would be a mistake. The last thing I want is to put her in any kind of danger, but there *is* someone who could help me.

Grabbing my phone from beside me on the mattress, I open up my texts and send out a message to Micah.

> Are you at the office today? ~Rebel

Within seconds, he reads it and three dots appear on my screen, indicating he's writing back.

> All day. Why? Need me? ~Captain Grumps

He has no idea how much I need him, all of him more than ever, and it runs deeper than the sexual response he evokes in me. I've always loved him, that's never gone away or dimmed, and right now, that's the only thing holding me up.

I want to be in his arms and find my peace. Need to feel more than this hollowness that's taken over my soul.

> Can I cash in last week's rain check and swing by? I need to talk to you about something. ~Rebel

For a beat, he doesn't reply. It just says read beneath my last message, but then his reply comes in and my sad heart gives a soft, happy thump. And while he might not mean it the way I wish he did, reading it again has a smile tugging at my lips.

> Come to me, sweetheart. I'm ready. ~Captain Grumps

Royce Cruise Lines looks exactly the same, and yet the moment I cross the lobby, the hairs on the back of my neck stand up. I've never felt uneasy here, but today I'm crawling with the need to turn around and walk right back out.

"What the hell?" I mutter under my breath, accepting a greeting from the girl who works the lobby's front desk. The word *condolences* meets my ears seconds after the call of my name, and I give her the same appreciative nod I've become a professional at giving.

Head tilt. Sad smile. Slow blink.

It's a combination people understand, and it stops them from probing with the follow-up question of *How are you holding up?*

I truly despise that. There's never going to be an answer of optimism or elation after losing someone you love, contrary to what my brother and Micah, or even Thiago, think. That stab of sadness will always be there.

"Liliana, hey!" I'm stopped from reaching the elevators by a smiling Beverly, and I give her a slow blink. We haven't interacted much after her demotion; her bitchiness isn't my cup of tea, and I have no idea what on my face reads *please come talk to me* at the moment. "I'm so sorry about—"

"Beverly, I'm really on a tight schedule and have Micah waiting for me. Can we continue this at another time?"

"I deserve that." She doesn't step aside, though. Instead, Beverly gets a little closer and gives my shoulder a squeeze while the happiness of a few minutes ago drops into an expression of sadness. "I've been an asshole to you, and I'd like to apologize. Can we talk for a minute? I promise it'll be quick, but after what happened to your father..."

As she droned on, I stopped listening after she mentioned my father. No one outside of his closest acquaintances knew about his passing, higher officials asked it to be that way for the ongoing investigation— saying he had a personal matter to deal with.

But somehow this woman whom I've barely exchanged words in

the past with has this knowledge? For that matter, how did the receptionist know?

I hadn't caught on to that. *The fuck?*

Did Micah tell the company? From the corner of my eye, I catch Ligo and Isaac talking, both oblivious to my being here, but I'm tempted to interrupt and ask how much they know.

And if they do, was it because of their security job or—

"…so can we?"

"I'm sorry, what?"

Beverly giggles, and both men look over, giving her a hard stare. Not both of us—just her. "So silly, Liliana. I was asking if we could step into the stairwell and talk for a moment. Away from prying eyes."

"Why? The real reason, Beverly."

"Because I have the answer to the questions you're asking yourself. Because there is a traitor—"

"Lead the way."

Maybe it's stupid and naïve for me to go with her, especially since we're out of sight, but at the moment, I'm running on impulse. To put it all behind me. To stop someone else from being hurt.

The stairs are seldom used in this building outside of employees wanting to make their step goals for the day, and I find the lighting to be too dim for my liking. *Micah needs to fix this.* It's warmer than the lobby, too, but none of that truly matters when we go up four flights before she stops in front of the exit door.

"It was never personal, you know," she says, head turned to look at me from over her shoulder. The same snide expression she's always worn is back in place, and the feelings of something being off return. I didn't listen to my intuition in the lobby. I let her take me out of a room full of witnesses and traded it for whatever this is. "You were just in my way. My aspirations in life aren't to be the glorified coffee maker for an executive, but to marry one, and that can't happen if he only has eyes for you."

"The hell are you babbling on about? Who's the traitor?" Instead of answering, Beverly knocks on the door three times before the handle turns and he steps through, smug satisfaction coming off him in waves. "Seriously? You?"

"Hello, Ms. Armas." Jeremy steps fully onto the landing, and in his hand there's a gun. "It's been a while since our last conversation...I do apologize for that."

"What the hell is this, Jeremy? What games are you playing at?"

"I'm just a man securing his future, Liliana." In the past, I saw him as just another man who faded into the background when in the presence of Micah. Nothing about him stood out to me, but after today, that will never be the case. "A future that you'll be helping me finance with that beautiful mind of yours. Because you truly are remarkable, Ms. Armas. It's been a pleasure watching you outgrow your peers these last few months, completely oblivious to how everyone looks at you."

"There's nothing special about her," Beverly hisses lowly from my left, and his eyes flash to hers. It's a slow movement, the lecherous expression on his face becoming dark hate as his gaze makes her shift back a step. "You said she was just a means to an end."

"I said whatever I needed to gain your compliance, Beverly," he sneers her name, his fingers twitching on the trigger of his gun. "But you were too stupid to see through that. Your vanity is your downfall."

"This isn't part of our agreement. Be done with her already."

"Know your place, bitch."

"There's a traitor in the Royce company, Liliana. He's been paid a lot of money—made promises by the same people responsible for the accident involving your father and brother. Be careful, honey. This isn't over."

"Because I need your help, Lili. So does Micah."

They spread the news because they knew about my father, and it wasn't because of Micah. Jeremy is who the person behind the transfers paid and made promises to. What they offered him, I don't know, but I have a feeling it has to do with my firewall project.

"You stole from me after I got you this job. I'm the reason you're here, Jeremy," I say, putting myself closer to the steps in case he decides to shoot. I'll take my chances stumbling down the stairs rather than making this easy for him. "That's really pathetic. Cowardly."

"Shut up."

"You took my work and tried to pass it off as yours, but you failed at that...didn't you? Did Micah turn down your pitch, or did the prototype you built fail?"

"Doesn't fucking matter now. It's my turn to have it all." His head's shaking as he follows, seeing my intent. Then, there's the silent threat not to move. "You'll sign the release to me and then I'll make you disappear, just like Uncle Joseph said. Sorry it has to be this way, Lili."

Is he talking about Joseph Wilburn? Dad's deputy mayor?

Jesus, this is horrible. Disgusting.

I think of each time that asshole ate dinner with us after being elected, and even beforehand. For a while, he was a regular while trying to run a successful campaign to be elected under my father as his second-in-command. Then, there was the slogan I provided to kick things off, doing anything I could to help them both.

Dad took him under his wing, and this is how he pays him back?

Betrayal is a bitter pill to swallow and right now, it tastes like acid. Flesh-destroying acid.

I don't show him how deep my anger runs, though. Instead, I keep my expression neutral and unbothered. "It does. The legal copyright was filed and granted to Liliana Armas, and last I checked, that's me."

It's a lie, but he doesn't need to know that. I'll handle the legality after.

"Don't make me hurt you, Liliana. Believe it or not, I respect you so much."

"I'm not afraid of you." It's the truth. I'll claw and bite and fight to survive.

"Will you just shoot her already?" Beverly snaps at him, and for a second I'd forgotten she was even here. *Who does she get in this? Jeremy, or Micah?* That question brings bitter jealousy to the forefront, and I'm tempted to wrap my hands around her neck for insinuating there could ever be a possibility between them. She'd never be worthy of him. "Quit wasting time and end this. They'll know she's missing by now, and Royce will come looking for her."

"Enough!" Jeremy waves the gun carelessly then; his inclination was to shoot, but he held himself back at the last minute. There's a nervous twitch in him, though. He's jumpy, and his right foot keeps tapping the ground the longer we stand where anyone can find us. It's speeding up, too. Eyes crazed. "Liliana, I'm going to need you to do as I say, and this will all be over soon. Be a good—"

He's cut off by the sound of multiple guns being cocked, and then the sudden blow from the door being kicked in behind him. This causes Jeremy to stumble and his finger on the trigger to press down, creating a loud bang inside the enclosed stairwell. My ears hurt from the sound, and the loud screech that follows is nothing short of horror-filled, yet nothing can take my attention away from the second bullet dislodging from Micah's gun.

It was almost in slow motion; the spark and then a sharp booming sound before the squelch of it entering Jeremy's head.

I'll always remember the crazed look in Jeremy's eyes when he first walked in.

I will forever remember the way the disgust rolled through my stomach when he gave me an appreciative look, making me feel dirty.

I'll never be able to forget the sound of part of his head being blown off seconds after the first body hit the floor.

Yet nothing registers more—burrows itself into my consciousness—than the dark look of satisfaction Micah wore while standing above his kill. He was a beast, not a man. A prideful monster that took in the two dead ex-employees before turning those same hooded blue eyes on me.

There was a fire there. Hunger and want.

Moreover, I can't look away while he dares me to—my entire body feels flushed and my lips part—thighs clenching beneath the long flowy skirt of the maxi dress I'd worn today. Then there's the way my nipples pebble into near-painful tips, throbbing behind the nonexistent cover of my sheer bralette that I'm quick to hide beneath crossed arms.

But more than that, I am attracted to the carnage bleeding out mere feet from me. A sick and twisted part of me feel vindicated, almost satiated, and I know he sees it, too.

It's why I back away as he begins to bark out orders I can't quite understand.

It's why when everything in me tells me to run, I listen.

Yet I heard him. The warning. The promise.

"Run, Liliana. Run and hide because I'm coming for what's mine."

Chapter 21
MICAH

Liliana's alone and completely unaware of the way I watch her from the other side of the open-access curved shower. No glass or door is needed. The space sinks down two steps and is deep enough to avoid spillage with two built-in-drains that don't allow water to seep out. Not that it matters to me if she floods the entire building with the way she is currently standing underneath the waterfall feature.

Eyes closed. Soaking wet.

Helpless while the jets from different angles massage her lithe frame in the dimmed light.

Slowly, she takes in shallow breaths—everything that happened today's finally catching up with her. Rebel watched me take a life.

Witnessed the depth of my darkness and obsession, two things I've always kept under control for her sake.

It no longer applies, though.

There are consequences for disobeying me, and I warned her just a few hours ago...

Run, Liliana. Run and hide because I'm coming for what's mine.

"Fuck." Four sinful letters, and they leave her on frustration-filled groan, this deep exhale as her body shivers and the blood on her skin drips down, mixing with the hot water as it sluices down her tan flesh. This is the first time I've fully seen her like this, enjoyed her curves—I've been blessed to be gifted such a pretty pussy as my reward for my years of patience. Devotion.

I'm going to bury my tongue deep inside her cunt, and the thrill and depravity of this hunt will only make the moment that much sweeter.

I want to corrupt her.

Own her in the same animalistic way she has me collared and prostrated at her feet.

She's my goddess, and her temple is my home.

"My sinful little rebel. Always so unafraid." My voice is low and gravelly, yet it doesn't carry over the sound of multiple showerheads hitting her body and the black-marbled walls. That, and I'm partially hidden within the low lighting and the mist of fog billowing and overtaking every inch of our personal playground, the latter of which she isn't aware.

Just as I know she wants this, too.

Two floors below ours and with a privately coded entrance, I built this luxury gym with her in mind. From a yoga room to every machine inside and then the large steam room she's visited once—the shower my Liliana is using to hide from me knowing I'd check her apartment first.

I did this for her. For our future enjoyment.

And no one has a key but us, something she hasn't picked up on yet, and it's been worth every penny. Every time she uses her keycard, I get the alert. Every room inside has a sensor that will always tell me exactly where she hides.

I will be her masseuse. I will fuck her into submission.

You were born to be mine, Rebel. Made from my rib and created to choke on my cock.

Shifting, Liliana stretches her neck from side to side while arching her back, and the sight has my cock throbbing painfully as I follow her every inhale as she shifts, highlighting the perky slope of each breast and the toned flesh of her abdomen. To me, it feels like a taunt. A silent dare as she reaches a dainty hand toward the wall where an always-filled shower gel dispenser sits.

Two pumps and she brings the soap toward the water, letting its scent fill the room. This earns a hum of pleasure from the both of us; the blend I'd commissioned to complement her scent of cupcake decadence mixes exquisitely, and I like the addition of strawberries and spun sugar.

It's a hint of tartness with her sweet cream. *So* fucking good, and to watch those small hands gather more and then rub together before spreading across her chest is the definition of heaven to me. They rub and squeeze, fingers sliding across each pebbled nipple until both are hard—goosebumps rising across her skin before they skim lower.

Down her abdomen and hips, from right to left, before stopping just over her mound. Then, she gyrates a bit, the move so fucking sexy, and I can't stop myself from releasing my cock and stepping out of the bloodied pants I never changed out of. They pool at my bare feet before I kick the fabric aside and take a step closer, then another, stroking my length lazily as I take in every second of the show before me.

How my girl rolls her voluptuous hips again.

How her lips part, a sinful gasp escaping.

My hips buck in time with her movements, my breathing accelerating as a growl builds inside my chest. One I bite back. *Not yet.*

Liliana opens her eyes a few seconds later and looks over at the bench to her left. This open shower is wall-to-wall and curves at the center with dual benches big enough to lie down on—get on all fours —on either side if you so desire. I designed the space myself, picked every single material used, and my one personal demand is I wanted it to be wide.

So she can stretch. Spread for me.

But motherfuck, the reality is so much better than my fantasies.

Rebel lifts one sinuous leg and places her foot flat against the dark marble, opening herself up for me. My eyes don't leave her curves, gliding across her satin skin, and then settle on the rosy bare flesh of her cunt with a single thin line of neatly trimmed hair just above her clit.

Pink and soft and mine, her pussy's dripping and I bet every cent I have to my name that it's not all soapy water. Not with the ease in which two fingers sink lower, and the smile tugging at her mouth is proof of that.

She enjoyed watching me kill Jeremy even if she doesn't understand why. I saw it back there, too.

Her lips curve into a smile and it's one that reminds me of the first time I kissed her. She wore the same cheeky grin that day. So devious yet innocent; a combination that makes no sense, and no one but her could pull off.

"You'll be the death of me, Micah." It's a whisper full of need, a calling out to me, and I respond with that low growl inside my chest I can no longer fight back. She doesn't hear it at first, nor does she see me, but the sudden tight grip of my hands on her hips causes her to freeze.

I'm behind her and pressed tight. My cock nestles against the small of her back while a hard shiver rushes through her small frame. She's as affected by me as I am by her, and when I trail my hands up her ribcage and cup a supple tit in each palm—she moans.

Low and throaty and the sound settles on the head of my cock, causing it to pulse. It jerks against her, pre-come slipping from the slit and onto her skin. I rub it against her. Marking her.

"You're mine, Liliana. Always have been." It's a guttural growl against her temple, my lips leaving gentle kisses between each word, a complete contrast to how I squeeze her breast—weighing and jiggling before tweaking each pebbled tip, an action that gifts me another of those delicious sounds. "I will honor, cherish, and fuck you like the precious treasure you are. My slut. My world. Mine."

"Jesus, Micah. I'm—"

"Loved beyond all measure, baby." With the tip of two fingers from my right hand, I slap each nipple and the top of her breast. Each strike is sharp, leaving just enough of a sting that she shakes in my hold but doesn't pull away. Instead, she presses herself closer after lowering her foot from the bench. Those beautiful light brown eyes meet mine through the thickening fog as she seeks my lips, turning her face toward me while rising onto the tips of her toes.

Her lips part, but no words come out. For a few seconds, Liliana watches me the same way I've enjoyed her from the shadows all these years. Salaciously. So much fucking hunger in those hazel orbs.

My perfect girl.

Hooded eyes and gasping little breaths escape her as she greedily breathes in my every exhale and it's when she whines for me, a lonely cry for my touch, that I lower my lips to hers.

This kiss isn't like any of the others we've shared. My hands roam her body, everywhere I can reach except her cunt, while my tongue plunders and strokes—claiming her. Her tongue twines with mine, desperate as she tries to take control, but I don't allow it.

I drag an open palm up her midsection and the center of her chest before reaching her throat, wrapping my fingers around the soft skin. Squeeze just a bit. Force her to stop moving.

"You're going to be patient, sweetheart." I lick the seam of her mouth. "Play under my rules for once."

"Please, Micah. Kiss me." Another keening sound. "I've been wanting this for so long."

"And I've been waiting on you just as long. I've always been here." This time, I peck her. Just slide my lips across hers while turning us and walking backwards until the back my legs touch the marbled bench. "Just like I'm going to give you the world, Rebel. Everything I've ever done has been for you. I'll also give you all my firsts. I've saved myself for you."

"You have? No one?" There's possessive pride in her tone, and it makes me feel like a king.

"I'd never touch or love anyone but you, my perfect little rebel."

Lowering us, I keep my hold firm as I lift her with the hand not on her throat, and then sit. She's on my lap facing away from me with her back to my chest, and I love the way she doesn't shy from spreading her thighs. Not enough, but I'm quick to remedy that by opening her further while placing each knee over one of my own.

Wide and needy. So perfect.

From my position, I have a clear view down her chest to her mound and the soft lips of her pink, slick flesh. Her slit is parted and her clit swollen; I cup her with one hand while the digits around her throat flex and then tighten. Rebel's pulse quickens under my touch while she once again turns her head as far as I allow.

She swallows hard as I press another slow kiss to her parted lips, slipping my tongue inside to twine with hers. At the first flick, she moans and those hips on my lap gyrate, fighting to find the release she craves while my cock pulses beneath her ass.

With each shift, her cheeks part and I'm nestled between them. Warm. "What do you need, Rebel. Tell me."

"All of you." No hesitation. No doubt.

"Good girl," I hiss from between clenched teeth as a rush of her warm juices soaks my hand and wrist, a few drops rolling down to her other hole. It makes it easier for me to slide against her, but it's not enough and I tap her thigh. "Rise a bit for me, love."

She does as I ask, lifting her lower half just enough that I'm able to bring my cock against her pussy. Press it there for a few seconds before I slide through her labia, from entrance to clit using my already wet hand, grip tight, until I'm covered in her slickness. Liliana trembles at this, thighs shaky as she holds herself just a few inches from my cock, and I can't help myself when I dip just the tip in.

Just a bit. The swollen head.

And while I know it'd be so easy to impale her on my cock, I don't.

I'm a man of my convictions, and her pussy will be a selfish gift on our wedding night.

Instead, I pull the tip out and tap myself against her clit twice in a soft kiss before moving back to her ass. I spread her juices there, sliding against each tight hole until she's writhing—from back to front until her thighs threaten to give out—before yanking her back onto my lap.

Her yelp makes me chuckle against her temple, but that quickly turns into a moan of my own as her asscheeks clench around me. I'm held tight against her, each flex massaging my length, and I return the favor by giving a single sharp slap to her bundle of nerves, then another as I tighten my hand on her throat, not enough to choke but to feel my control, pulling a deep and guttural cry from her lips.

"Micah!"

"I'm here, baby." Every single muscle in Rebel's body stiffens while pleasure overtakes her senses, and her orgasm is a thing of beauty. She flushes and shivers, thighs jerking while I now rub her through each ripple, her come so slick between my fingers. "Trust me. Let me love you."

"I'm yours." Her truth. My honor. "And I've always loved you."

"Thank you." Prolonging her release, I slip two fingers inside her to the first knuckle. She's so wet and warm, tight around my fingers, but still bucks against me. Deeper, and I feel her innocence.

I caress the soft flesh. Gentle and slowly, pushing a little but not breaking it.

Another small gush slips through my fingers and spreads, runs down to her ass, and coats us both. I'm still rocking against her, loving the feel of her but I don't come.

Not yet. The next time I do, it'll be inside of her. *Her ass is mine.*

"You didn't…?"

"This wasn't about me, Rebel. Only you."

Liliana's languid in my hold now. I release her throat and stop petting her, helping her stand and move back underneath the warm water. She lets me wash her and help rinse, only lifting her arms long enough to wipe something off my chin.

And when she moves her fingers just far enough that I'm able to see, I wait.

Yet she doesn't react to the blood. Not how I expected, at least, after she watched me kill a man.

Instead, she crooks those same fingers, and I lower my face down to her level. For a minute or two, we don't talk—not so much as blink—but I'm made to feel a hundred feet tall when she whispers three words.

"Always been you."

There's a serious conversation pending between her and I, but for now, I'm happy to enjoy this moment. To burn into my memory every sinful bloodlust-induced moment like what we just experienced. Led by desire and the pride in taking out her enemy—she felt it too—and we gave in to every restrained desire we've held back for so long.

I didn't claim her innocence yet or gave her my first time, but I showed her who she belongs to.

It's not a streak of blood on my cock that will prove it, but how deeply I worship her. Sweet. Filthy. It doesn't matter when both sides of me are hers.

We're real. Perfect for the other, and it shows in how easily we move together and take pleasure from a simple kiss.

But that can wait until tomorrow. For now, I'll be tucking her into my bed where she's always belonged.

"It's time to go home, baby."

Chapter 22
LILIANA

H e's the one constant in my life.

My love for him has never waned, and I've never been more at ease than I am laying naked in his arms, wrapped tightly in an embrace that's starting to mend my broken heart.

Everything's not perfect. Moving on from grief takes time, but I won't deny that for the first time in my life, I feel like I'm where I truly belong.

This is a man who's never left my side, nor does he hinder my need to grow. Who will understand this insatiable need to pay tenfold for what's been taken from our family.

Everything will be okay?

Is this what they meant? That he does love me?

"Have I been blind this entire time?" His arm tightens around my midsection and his cock gives a jerk from between my thighs. We're pressed chest to back without an inch of space between us and each time I shift, Micah follows, keeping himself semi-hard against my pussy lips.

My labia that's slick with my arousal and dripping down his length as he flexes in his sleep. He doesn't do it constantly, but just enough that I'm kept horny and the flesh there has become sensitive.

My clit throbs against him.

My mound feels swollen.

And I know that if I were to move, grind against his girth, I'd come. It would take so little. Just one small swivel of my hips and...

"You need to wake up, Micah," I coo, but he continues to ignore me, and the little snore that follows is adorable. Endears him to me a little more, even if this predicament is all his fault.

Yet that doesn't negate the fact he's been using my pussy to keep warm.

"Okay. Two can play this game." A smile tugs at my lips when I shift and hear his grunt of annoyance. Those strong, corded arms tighten, one around my hips and the other grips my neck. It's a reflex; I have no idea how he's comfortable nearly cocooning me—wrapped around my much smaller frame like a blanket—but at the tap of my fingers on his hand, he lets go.

He's asleep but attuned to me, and I won't deny it's a heady feeling. Being the center of his attention always has been.

In the past, he never allowed anyone to get close enough to flirt, much less ask me out. No buying me coffee while in line at Starbucks. No making small talk at a bookstore where I waited for the store employee to come back with my pick-up order.

He's pussy-blocked me for years, and I'd been oblivious this entire time.

But now that my eyes are open, his actions were always possessive. Of ownership, a privilege he gave me in return.

I always had unlimited access to him. To every facet of his life.

"Captain Grumps deserves a reward."

As if he heard me, that hand still on my hip tightens, sending a tiny lick of pleasure between my legs. We haven't had sex, but when he slipped the engorged head of his cock inside of me last night, I felt a small bit of stretch. He's thick and long while I'm small, and even if the way I clench in desperation indicates I want to be ridden hard, I know he's going to ruin me.

Yet I won't deny that the thought excites. He's going to be my first, as I will be his.

It's a precious privilege that Micah waited for me; I've always been what he wants. Knowing that he hungered for me all this time...

"*Fuck,* Papi. I love you," I whisper against his neck, leaving a series of small kisses down and then across his collarbone. He smells a little like me mixed with that citrusy bourbon, and I find myself aroused by the sweet yet tart scent. It's us. Ours.

Another minute shift and I'm able to slip a little beneath the covers, his hand at my waist slipping upwards, the pads on his fingers dragging up my side and the outside of my breast until I'm face to semi-hardness, lips a few inches above the head.

My mouth waters at the sight; he's perfection in the male form, and I can't help but trace the slit at the top with my tongue. Softly. Feather light.

God, my body thrums at the first taste of him with a little bit of me, and my core clenches; I can't stop the shiver that crests down my spine nor the way my nipples tighten. They swell and throb, my entire body coming alive as he infiltrates every one of my senses.

His body heat.

His scent.

His salty-sweet essence.

I can't help or stop the groan that slips past my lips, and I do it again. Longer this time, flicking the tip where beads of pre-come pool for me and I lap each one, flushing as his cock hardens to full mast. So hard. It flexes in my grip, and I wrap my lips fully around the head and suck, wanting—needing more of the addictive pearl-like drops.

I can see why women say kneeling for a man is addictive. Almost an art form.

The power it gives you. The rush of endorphins when you hear that first groan from your male before the sheets are ripped off the bed and his hooded eyes meet yours.

This my nirvana.

Hedonistic bliss.

"Rebel, fuck, baby." His tone is husky. Deeper and warm from sleep. "What—"

"I'm busy, Mr. Royce," I say around him, but then release him with a pop. I've never done this before, but the nerves never show up. I've read plenty of romance novels and watched countless hours of porn like most women do, and the act itself is pretty self-explana-tory. Yet none of that matters. Loving this man and wanting to give him all of me is instinctual.

A compulsion I follow blindingly while dragging the flat of my tongue down the underside to the base and nuzzle the flesh there. His scent is deeper here, concentrated, pure Micah, and I kiss my way to his balls before sucking the right one into my mouth.

I'm not stroking him, not even holding him in a tight grip. No. This is me worshipping him with my mouth the way he always cares for me.

It's the little ways. Subtle yet important, going as far as to drink coffee how I do because I'm making it for him.

That's love. That's complete adoration.

Why did it take me so long to realize this?

Releasing the right one, I take the left and show it the same affec-tion. Softly, I suckle his testicle—licking, nipping, and pulling it into my mouth.

He growls at me for this, the sound so male, a needy calling that I answer with a moan. I love the taste and feel of him, my hands gripping my breasts and squeezing while I work my parted lips up the side and back toward the velvet tip. I'm pinching my nipples as I take him in my mouth, sucking him down about halfway before pulling back to breathe.

"Again. Suck me again." A guttural command and I follow it, opening my mouth wide while holding my tongue out. I like the feel and weight of him, how soft the tight skin is—I bob my head more, forcing more of his length inside, and choke. My eyes water, but I don't pull back. "*Motherfuck,* Liliana. So good. Your mouth is so warm and eager."

My response is a hum around his girth. I refuse to release him. Instead, I remember how every romance I've read says to relax. To enjoy it and breathe through my nose.

So I do just that, letting my body guide me, and I'm rewarded by another salty-sweet drop of pre-come. It bigger than the others, and I reward him by taking him in deeper for the gift.

I make it to just about an inch from the base before I find myself yanked off and airborne, almost slammed on my back with an angry Micah hovering above me.

He's breathing hard, lip curled over his teeth in a snarl while I can't stop myself from fluttering my lashes at him. I've never seen him like this before, and I like it. How he watches me from beneath hooded eyes—the heat in those blue orbs.

"I need you to know something, Liliana. I'm not taking this as a one-off or a moment of weakness." His mouth lowers to mine, almost touching. "You've been my world since the moment I met you, Rebel. Everything I am and will ever be is for you. Nothing comes before or matters more than you. This is real."

That fog of lust I'd been under calms for a moment, and my eyes tear up. These are things I've always yearned for him to say, but to actually have him…

"For me, it's always been you, too." That's all I can muster up, a little choked up by the softening of his expression. How he finally presses his warm lips against mine in the softest and sweetest of kisses.

That rush I felt a few minutes ago is still there, but it's more now.

Since waking up, I've been remembering his promises last night, hoping for this, but I didn't want to think—

"Everything I said last night is my truth, sweetheart. I want to fuck you into submission and then spoil you like the perfect princess you've always been to me. You're my world, Liliana, and I intend to spend the rest of my life showing you this." His tongue traces my lips, then slips inside to taste me. A groan leaves him, the sound settling on my swollen clit and my hips buck, causing him to chuckle. "Woke up needy, baby?"

"Yes."

"Yes, what? Tell me, sweet thing." This time, his kiss is hungrier than the last, and it holds that same dark edge of possessiveness I felt from him last night.

It leaves me breathless, yet craving more.

"I want you to kiss me just like that while buried deep inside of me. I want you to own me like you did last night."

Micah bites his bottom lip, eyes appraising my face. "Are you sure?"

"I am. Always been yours, Micah."

"And I will always love you." His voice is thick with arousal, his body thrumming with need. "I'm going to need your permission here, Liliana. I won't claim your pussy until our wedding next month, but I do need your approval for me to fuck your ass instead."

His words send a shockwave of unbridled desire through. One, because he wants to marry me. Two, because I'd never envisioned wanting to give myself so completely to a man.

I never thought I'd ever be pinned beneath Micah while he asks for my permission to take what I so willingly give.

It's sexy how he patiently waits for my answer. How he tries to persuade me by rubbing the head of his cock through my lips and up to my clit, each bump to the bundle of nerves sending a jolt of plea-sure through me.

Like a kiss. A quick peck.

And on the third run across my clenching hole and folds, I throw my head back and moan.

"Is that a yes, Rebel? Use your words."

"Dammit, yes. Please." I writhe against him, chasing an orgasm he denies me a second later. Not that I'm given time to complain; Micah flips my position, and I find myself face down and knees spread apart on my next blink. "Oh, fuck."

"I plan to."

"Soon?"

"Patience, Mami." The Spanish nickname rolls off his tongue and across my every processor. It floods my system with dopamine, manifesting physically in the wetness coating the top of each thigh.

I want to close them, rub them together, but his large hand cups me in a harsh grip, stopping any attempt. As does the way he pulls me back with those firm fingers and I follow, rising onto all fours with my ass high in the air.

"Beautiful." He emits a low groan while his hard cock rests against the cleft of my ass. He bucks a few times, just feels me, but then he's reaching a hand out toward his side drawer. In all the years he's lived here, I've never explored his penthouse, choosing to stay within what I consider safe spaces. His living room. Kitchen. The layout appears to be identical to mine, darker in furniture where I've always appreciated lighter colors and décor, but then my curiosity is forgotten when I hear the pop of a lid and a second later, there's a cool trickle of something slippery gliding down my clenching holes.

The sensation is new, and I won't deny that I like it. Enjoyed it when he rubbed himself against me there last night, dragging the head of his cock from pussy to ass and back again, but never more than that.

Yet the sensations as he did so were euphoric. Sharp little bites of pleasure that didn't last long enough teased my senses and forced me to arch my body in his hold—want more—but the sting of penetration always evaded me.

Because I know it will hurt. First times just do, and no matter which of my holes he claims today, my reaction would been the same. I'm at ease because it's Micah.

There's no tensing or fear, nothing but this slow warming sensation that's building as he touches me.

"You're the only thing that's perfect in my world. The only thing that's always been right." Micah curls himself over my back, his breath fanning the back of my neck. "Thank you for trusting me, Liliana. For this honor."

"It's your first time too." Breathy. A little whine. "You waited for me."

"And it's the best decision I ever made." Slowly, he pushes the pad of a thick finger inside, and it stings as it stretches out the ring of muscle past my entrance. Each pump of his finger hurts at first, the intrusion foreign, but behind the pain there's love in the way he kisses my shoulder blades, left then right, before returning his attention to my ass.

He pours more lube and spreads it.

Makes me a slick mess from pussy to ass, and I moan when his other hand massages my clit. He's gone from hovering behind my body, each entrance exposed in this position, to my left where he continually fingers me.

My ass clenches as his finger slides deeper until it's fully inside, and I'm left squirming and pushing against his hands. Clit swollen and throbbing, I pulse—

"Micah, what…oh!"

"Good girl. Relax" He's added a second finger, working both in slowly to draw out my pleasure. Between the penetration and the tight circles on my clit I'm trembling, moving my body in sync with his movements.

It's like the feeling of his hand around my neck last night. There's this edge of panic as your breathing is slightly cut off; it fights against the pleasure for dominance, but together they create this overwhelming strike of euphoria that's beautiful.

This has a touch of that in it. There's discomfort from the intrusion, but beneath it is this uncontrolled strike of rapture that I'm quickly becoming addicted to.

"That's it, Rebel. Come for me, sweetness." My body stopped being my own at the first sink of his fingertips. I'm not in control, and I release on command. Everything becomes too much and I'm screaming my release, unable to comprehend anything past *fuck* and *so good* and *Micah.* The latter is my prayer, and like the god he is, my love answers.

I feel him there. Sinking in slowly, testing my level of comfort as he pumps leisurely. No rush or craze to pump a few times and come like I've heard other girls claim their first times to be.

Instead, I'm treated like the princess he promised I'd be.

But maybe I want to be his slut, too.

Needing him deeper, I arch my back and spread my thighs a little wider for him. His responding grunt is heaven to my senses. "Just like that, baby. Motherfuck, you're tight and feel so good—perfect fucking ass."

"Yes. Yours," I grit out, so full and he's not all the way in. "More."

"Are you sure you can handle it?"

"More, Micah. All of you."

"That's my girl." Dragging himself out, he lays down on his back before lifting me like I weigh nothing. I'm placed where he wants me, straddling his hips and with the tip of his thick cock right against my rosebud. "Lower yourself. Show me how mine you are."

I swallow hard and nod, using my hand to guide him inside slowly. The temptation to drop myself is there, but I follow his earlier lead, just with circular motions.

A little more each time. Stopping when my knees shake so he can take over from below and with his arms crossed behind my back, riding me with sharper thrusts with the half we managed to get inside.

I'm not ready for the small burst of pleasure to become an electric wave that this angle brings. My chest is against his. My lips hover over his while every thrust makes me languid in his hold, and I just give in.

He overtakes me completely and the further I relax, the deeper and harder he begins to fuck me. Now this is him claiming me, not allowing me to move—all I can do is just feel and take.

His love. His desire for me.

"You're close, Rebel. I can feel you tightening around me while your cunt clenches at nothing." He's speaking into my parted lips; I can't do anything but breathe and hold on. "It needs to be filled by me. I'll be the only man to ever have you like this and experience the gift you are."

"Micah, I'm—"

"I know. Let go, love." One of the hands holding me down slips between us and touches my entrance—the one place after today he hasn't claimed yet. "The day you say *I do* to me in front of your family and friends, I'm going to stretch you to the point of pain. This sweet little hole…" he presses just a little deeper and I clench hard "…will be bred and marked by the end of the night, my wife. You're going to spend a lifetime always full of me."

That promise is my undoing.

I buck in his grip as my orgasm rock through me, stealing the very air from my lungs as I seat myself fully on his dick. To the hilt, gyrating as the feeling of being full, and owned, intensifies my pleasure, and a second later he comes with me.

Micah holds me in place and throbs, each pulse filling me to the brim, locking it inside until he moves. Which he never does.

There's no pulling out, just a slow and gentle roll of his hips beneath me while I lay atop his chest. I don't complain when he situates me to his liking or his left leg begins to rock in between the lazy fuck he continues to give me.

It actually lulls me, and I'm almost asleep when something hits me.

Using my arms to push up a bit since he's refusing to let me go, I narrow my sleepy eyes. "Wait a minute. Shouldn't you be asking permission to marry me? Where's my proposal?"

"I did propose." Micah has the gall to look offended. "My words were loud and clear."

"Liar. Ask me nicely, and I'll consider."

"No."

"No?"

"Yes." The hand that had been squeezing my ass now has a grip on my messy hair, pulling me down toward his lips. "I told you to run, Liliana. Run and hide, because I was coming for what is mine."

Chapter 23
LILIANA

The next time I wake up, Micah's side of the bed is cold and so am I.

He's covered my body in a soft, dark bedsheet—what looks to be midnight blue or black—and the curtains are closed. I can't tell what time of day it is, nor can I see much of what's in front of me, so I close my eyes and fight to cling to the last dregs of my sleep.

Not that it works, as the more aware I become, the colder I get.

It starts at my shoulders at first, but then slithers lower until my feet are ice-cold and I'm getting cranky. Without coffee first thing, I'm not a chipper person in the least.

"Should've just dragged him to violate me back on my bed. At least I'd have a comforter or be between blankets." There's nothing in the world I hate more than cold feet or hands. It ruins this, the safety roll I've started, how I'm tightening my burrito-like protection in hopes of rewarming myself, but stop when the pad of feet gets closer.

And closer.

Then, I feel his body heat near my hip, and it takes everything in me not to moan.

"I know you're awake, Rebel."

"I'm not." Denial's best served when I'm pre-caffeinated. I can't be held responsible for the checks I try to cash before my fix. "Please come back after you have what I need."

"Who says I don't?" One of his strong hands runs from my calf to ass and back down again, and I can't deny that warmth spreads throughout my body from his simple touch. I want more. Him all over again. "It wouldn't take much have you screaming for me again."

Opening one of my eyes, I peer at him. "That sounds like big talk, Mr. Royce."

"Want to make a bet?"

"What will I win?"

"Cocky much?"

"Always." My shrug is barely noticeable, so I stick a hand out and wave it around. He gets the gist and smirks, biting his bottom lip to keep from laughing. "Now, I'll ask again. What. Do. I. Win?"

"You asked for it, Lili." It takes a moment for my brain to register he called me a nickname that means *I'm in trouble* or *It's serious,* and this time, I believe it's a mixture of both. The sheet is ripped from my body and I bounce on the bed, yelping as the cold air hits every inch of my nakedness face up. "What the…Micah, wait!"

"Warned you, baby." His words are already muffled by my pussy as he licks me with the flat of his tongue, roughly parting my lips as a near-feral growl rumbles up his chest. There's no way to explain his action but he feasts on me, licking and nipping and slipping the tip of his tongue into my tight entrance to savor every bit of the wetness he pulls from me.

I'm wet and feel the ache and yearning for more.

I'm sore, but accept his finger in my other entrance with a squeal while gripping his hair. The feel of his mouth on me is indescribable, as amazing as what we did last night, and I want to do it all over again. Clenching around his tongue and digit, my body comes alight with that tease of an orgasm I chase but he takes away from me.

And he's smug about it. Chuckling at the look of heated betrayal I gift him, but all I get in return is a sharp nip to my thigh. "What do you want, Rebel? I thought there was nothing I could do for you?"

"No games, Papi. Please, no games."

"But you're so beautiful like this. All soft and needy."

"Micah!" It's a scream of frustration. Almost angry, but the sexy bastard just raises a brow before lowering his mouth to my pussy. This time, he's kissing me there. Sucking my labia and clit, alternating between the two—I can't do anything but grip his hair and try to hold him in place. A plan that fails the second he rakes his teeth over the area just above my clit, a hair's breadth from the trembling bundle of nerves, but it's as if he shocked me. Pleasure slams through my body and I'm thrusting my hips, riding his finger as ripple after ripple courses through every cell in my body until I fall back, panting.

I'm not even sure when I sat up, arching and bucking, but now I can't move.

"Better than the best cup of coffee that ever percolated in this caffeine-obsessed world."

"Is that so?"

"Yes, Papi." A little wheezing. "You did so good."

"That's what—" He's cut off by the ringing of his cell, and he reaches into his back pocket with one hand while wiggling the finger in my ass with the other. That little action makes me keen and I narrow my eyes at him, but before I can say anything, he answers. "Royce speaking."

It's on speaker, and heavy breathing comes through the line. I arch a brow at him, but he shrugs and waits. And waits.

We're left listening to what sounds like the sound of busy traffic and someone who's run a marathon.

"Speak, or I'm hanging up."

"Mr. Royce, I'd like to discuss a recent message left for me by your office. Two of them, actually." The voice is polite and male, definitely older, and Micah isn't surprised. If anything, his amusement turns into another come-hither movement with that blasted finger he refuses to remove, and I have to bite down hard on my lip in order not to groan. "Mr. Royce, are you there?"

"I'm here, just not interested. Wasn't I clear enough with Amado and Ricardo Vega?"

"Crystal. However, Micah, your father and I—"

"Have no relationship, personal or business, and I want your head on a fucking pike. So, unless this is to tell me where I can pick you up, don't waste my time."

"This is business, son. Nothing personal. What happened to Joaquin and Lilia—"

"I want you to listen to me, and listen very carefully, Rodolfo. Nothing is ever what it seems…" as he speaks, those beautiful blues stare into mine and there's something he's trying to convey but I'm missing "…and I'm coming for you. Enjoy your last few days breathing."

"Micah, it—" He doesn't let him finish, choosing to hang up then and toss the phone aside before sweeping me up with his unoccupied hand. His other finger is still inside me. I'm a mess again after the quick wipe-down he gave me before I passed out, and it lasted only long enough to clean me and then bury his semi-hard cock back into my tender back entrance.

That's how we slept.

A part of him always touching me. In me.

And I like it.

Has a certain appeal that makes my mouth water and an idea blossom.

"You have no idea the kind of monster you're creating, Mr. Royce."

"Is that so?" My response is a nod and then a pout of my lips as we enter his large en-suite bath. Against the wall and near the windows, there's a custom built-in tub big enough to fit his frame and other people. At the very least three, and I'm suddenly in the mood for a long and hot soak. Something I plan to tell him, but then he's walking toward it while planting small kisses along my cheek. "Can I make a request, though?"

"Of course."

"Good." Now his lips are by my ear, exhaling roughly while slipping something onto my ring finger. It's cold, heavy, and leaves me speechless—tears brimming my eyes at the sight of an engagement ring with a purple diamond at the center. *When did he*— "Because I want my personal little devil to be a brat at times, too. I truly do love that sassy mouth of yours."

One Month Later...

Micah

THE HEAVY SOUND of my boots carries through the staff *highway* on a friend's ship.

There's no one around, and the usual hustle and bustle on a vessel this size and with the kind of clientele that likes to cruise down the Mediterranean, it's costing the owner a pretty penny.

But then again, for a man worth billions, this isn't but a blip in the system, and I appreciate it dearly. Because for over a month now these assholes have evaded me, but the vacation ends here.

Especially when the older Diaz decided to insult the owner's wife over a lost game of poker.

He didn't know who they were at first—traveling under a false passport and name helped—but drunken men don't know how to bite their tongues. His insult turned into threats and the promise to do the same to him as they'd done to Joaquin.

Big mistake. Life ending.

Eugene Karlson is a friend. An old investor when the company was first established under my father, and he stayed on the board only long enough to see it succeed, recoup his earnings, and move to Italy where his wife is from.

His call came at the perfect time, too. Liliana's been a little stressed with our wedding plans, and I don't know why, to be honest. All she needs to find is the dress.

Everything else is planned out according to the Pinterest board she started when we were teens. I've always had access to it, and made notes whenever her taste changed. From blood red to pink—to now classic white and black with touches of gold.

She claims it reminds her of how different our styles are and I agree, but we could've been married in a Pepto pink explosion and it wouldn't have mattered. Her happiness is what drives me. Knowing it'll be my ring on her finger when the night is through—and I'm wearing her blood on my cock like a badge of honor—is my only input in the preparations.

Something I've easily remedied by purchasing an island to hold our family and host the celebration, while Esmeralda will be docked and ready to leave the next day with our wedding guests. We'll have another boat to christen, something sleek and fun, and I plan to enjoy watching my wife sunbathe in the nude or riding my cock under the stars.

But not yet. That's not why I'm here.

Brian and Rodolfo Diaz are on the other side of the door that leads the staff into the dining room and are scrambling back, stumbling over themselves while I grin. If anything, you'd say they've seen the face of the devil and are now reborn believers in faith.

The problem is the wicked never make it into the kingdom of heaven.

And these men are sinners. Filth.

It's also safe to say they're not happy to see me, but I'm pleased to find them well, and now the older of the two is nursing what looks to be a broken nose. Rodolfo handles a punch better than his son.

Testament to that is the blood dripping down his shirt while he remains upright.

He deserves everything coming his way, but nothing will ever be more satisfying than watching Liliana land one on him. She doesn't wait for my signal, storming past me and right up to the asshole, cocking her arm back then landing a solid blow to his nose. The sound of broken bone is instant, and she smiles sweetly at that while shaking out her hand.

Rivulets of red rush from the wound while he howls, Brian trying to intervene as I step inside, but one kick to his kneecap and he folds like a chair. All bark, no bite.

"Stand up, Brian."

"Royce, it was just business. None of this was personal." Rebel scoffs at Rodolfo from beside me, already moving toward him to land another well-deserved blow, but I haul her back by the waist of her denim shorts and shake my head when she looks back at me from over her shoulder.

Liliana's stressed, and it shows. I've learned over the last few months that sometimes a time-out is all she needs to settle and regain control of herself.

I know what will help her. Will handle her in a minute.

"You made a horrible mistake, Rodolfo. You played your hand, and now I'll play mine."

Isaac, Ligo, and Alfred are there to intervene the moment I turn my back on them and walk away with the woman who owns my cock and soul. They have their instructions and Alfred will have paid his debt soon enough, dirtying his hands alongside Ligo who's teaching him how to stop being a fuck-up.

I take us out of the room and back up toward the suite provided for our time here. There's no foreplay or sweet words needed right now. She knows what she wants, and I take my place on a chair she asked the staff to provide for the room.

Delicate hands unzip my pants and reach in, pulling out my cock; I'm already half-hard for her and give a small jerk against her lips right before she suckles me. I'm taken into her mouth while she kneels on the carpet, relaxing against me while her tongue moves beneath the underside.

It's beautiful how she finds comfort in me. How with every slow suck or just the feel of me on her tongue, she loses rigidity until my pliant and happy girl is back.

We stay like that for a while, me playing with her hair until her eyes finally find mine.

"You okay, sweetheart?"

"Frustrated," she speaks around my girth. It's a little muffled, but I understand. "Can't find a dress I like."

"Is that it?"

"My hand hurts, too."

"How bad?" My answer is met with a shrug, and I flick her forehead. "Answer me."

"That hurt, you know."

"Good. Now answer."

"Three out of ten on the pain scale."

"Okay. I'll get you some Ibuprofen in a minute." Cupping the underside of her jaw, I thrust up and force her head down so she chokes on my cock a bit. Drool slips from her mouth to the base, and I love the way her eyes water. *So pretty.* "Tomorrow we'll go shopping for a dress and if we still find nothing, then we'll hire someone to design whatever you envision. And two, I want you to go and bend over the vanity for me, baby. I'm going to fuck that pretty little ass until you cry for me. I'm here to provide for you, and that includes breaking a few bones if you desire. Never hurt yourself again, understood?"

"Yes, Papi."

"And no complaining when the onboard physician checks it out after, either."

"Yes, boss."

"Good girl."

Epilogue 1
LILIANA

∞♥

THREE MONTHS LATER...

The first time I dreamed of the day I'd get married; this wasn't the scenario I envisioned.

As a kid, I wanted that fairy-tale wedding that comes at the end of all princess movies. The kind where you meet the man of your dreams at the end of a grand aisle and say *I do* before a priest. You'd profess your undying love for each other by waxing poetic lyrics about being a better person, heartbeats fluttering when your eyes meet, and every emotion a person can put into a singular speech.

Yet the reality of this day is so much better than anything I could have ever imagined.

Because standing before me and ready to walk me down the

"dock" is a man I thought I'd never see again. He's a little thinner now and is walking with a cane; my father smiles at me with my mother beside him, and both have tears in their eyes.

Our closest friends and family are here today to celebrate with us, too. They've been arriving since yesterday, flying into the private airstrip on this lush tropical island my husband purchased as a wedding gift to me. A piece of the Virgin Islands we can come back to throughout the years for our anniversary or a family vacation with the brood of children we want to have.

He wants six. I say four.

"You look beautiful, Lili. Preciosa." Hearing his tone as I get closer brings everything into reality, and I can't help the small, happy sob that escapes me. I'm hugging him close and rocking side to side, still not quite believing what I'm seeing.

"How?" Pulling back, I bring his hand to my cheek. "I thought you—"

"Micah saved my life."

"And nothing is ever as it seems," I add with a watery laugh, their behavior making so much sense now. The looks accompanying the saying. The disappearing act my mother made shortly after Lionel woke up. *Nothing is ever truly as it seems.*

Micah said it.

Lionel said it.

Thiago said it.

Even my mother, in her own way, told me she needed to leave to mend her heart. That one day I'd understand—I do.

"Are you upset?" Dad asks, and my response is an immediate no. How can I be? I'm being gifted a second chance at a relationship with him and my mom. How many people would give just about anything for a single moment with a loved one, and I'd be the biggest asshole to spit in Micah's face for protecting those I love.

"I'm not." My bottom lip wobbles, and I bite it. Try to control my tears and not ruin my makeup, and I'm thankful when Luna steps forward and, using a napkin, wipes under my eyes. "Thank you."

"No bride should be upset on her wedding day."

"I'm blessed, not upset. So freaking blessed." I'm sure someone will fill me in on the how later, but at that moment, I can't help but look behind me and toward the pier where our boat is docked. *Rebelde* is my soon-to-be husband's new toy, and the luxury yacht will be where I'll tie myself to him for the rest of our lives.

When we first started planning this wedding, I thought having a board with ideas and color schemes and absolute perfection was all that mattered. But it was when we found my dress—we visited every available shop in Miami and surrounding cities—that my desires changed.

In a small couture shop in the downtown area owned by a lovely Brazilian woman, I fell in love.

Unconventional and sexy, the two-piece gown gave me a sense of thrill when I modeled it for my groom. I don't believe in bad luck or other mumbo-jumbo meant to take the fun out of the day.

The darkening of his eyes as I took everything off and slipped into the skin-tight lace top with a high neckline and cap sleeves made me clench my thighs mid-shop. The grunt of approval when the white tulle skirt with a high slit followed, gliding up my thighs and stopping over hipbones, leaving a small gap uncovered between garments, made me slick.

Hungry. Thankful.

I sucked his dick in the parking lot in appreciation for his help and was later gifted a full-body massage and a slow fuck in the ass.

But that day changed things. No more big ceremony; that's just for us. Our family and friend's can have the party. The moment my father hands me off, they'll walk back to eat, drink, and dance while we head out to sea.

"I love you guys, but I'm ready."

"Then let's go, Mamita. Let's walk you to your forever."

And they do. It's a slow procession with my father's cane, but I don't mind. I'm surrounded by love as we reach the end of the pathway to our dock where Micah's waiting for me, in his hand a single white rose to match my dress.

He's wearing white linen pants and a shirt, the sleeves rolled up to his elbows. Like me, he's barefoot, but there's a black piece of fabric around one ankle, and it's not until I'm closer that I realize what it is.

The ponytail holder might not mean anything to anyone else, but I find it adorable. It's his something old, like his watch on my wrist is mine.

The new is the matching tattoos on our ring fingers; one side has the date we met and the other, the day we wed.

I don't want perfect. Just him.

I don't want to make promises. Just cherish our bond.

Once we're within reach, Micah takes my hand and lifts it to his lips. "You look beautiful."

"Thank you, my little thief."

We walk away leaving our families behind with a promise to be back, and they watch us reach our boat where Micah's parents are waiting. They're there to help me on so I don't snag my dress before they rejoin the others.

"Go be happy," his mother whispers to me before her husband kisses my forehead and I'm handed over to my husband.

We're sailing out to international waters, deep enough that this will be a private ceremony between man, God, and three men who haven't seen the light of day in weeks.

For our ceremony, Micah ordained himself because we didn't want anyone else with us. Just the sea and a warm sunset while we feed the local fish.

It takes a while to reach international waters, but in between soft petting and the occasional warning to *behave,* we make it just in time.

After finding this place and buying it, we'd taken a smaller boat out to explore. Just like today, we drove toward the back end of the island and out to sea, meeting the same beautiful sight. There's a pod of orcas here, not common for this area at all, but the locals from a neighboring island told us they'd first been sighted last year.

The four adults and two cubs are gorgeous and sleek, playful as they come close to the boat. To explore. Test us out, and have even splashed me once in the past.

And while I know they don't eat humans; they'll play with them. Bite. Chew. Toss the three tied-up idiots around like beach balls and then leave them for other predators to feed on.

There are plenty of sharks that will come around later, and if nothing else, nature will take its course and they'll disappear into the warm waters never to be seen again.

My heart holds no empathy for them.

"You ready?"

"Born to be yours."

Nodding, Micah stands from the captain's chair, and together we walk down a short flight of stairs and onto the top deck. That's where they're huddled, sitting with their backs against the boat's wall while shivering—watching our every move with interest.

After weeks of being held captive inside Esmeralda, we had them transported on the same ship. It'll be taking off from St. Thomas and tour the Caribbean with our loved ones. The boat has permission to spend the night there for free as a wedding gift to us.

I walk to the back of the yacht and turn to look at my husband, who's busy standing the three men up. They shake and shiver, crying beneath the tape covering their mouths but then that turns to screams of pain when it's suddenly ripped off.

"Plead your case."

Brian is the first, blubbering. "We've suffered enough, Mr. Royce. Please let me go. I was just following orders."

"No." In the blink of an eye, he's been kicked in the chest and falls overboard, the splash from his body meeting the water sounding painful. "Next."

"Micah, she wasn't touched. Joaquin was unfortunate, but you have her, at least."

"They don't know?" He shakes his head, and I giggle. "This will be good."

"Tell them, Liliana. They have a right to know." Their attention is pinging back and forth, desperate and lost looks on their faces.

"My father is alive."

"How? But all this time…no!" Joseph will never learn the truth as he follows Brian down, screaming the entire way until—nothing. Either the impact has knocked the wind out of both or they're hurt, but I don't waste my time to look.

"Speak up." He's the one Micah's most angry at, cracking his neck side to side. "Give me your plea."

"Why?"

"Because since the moment I met this woman, I vowed to never let anyone hurt her, and you came close to doing so." He takes a step closer to Rodolfo, taking his shirt off in the process. It drops to the ground, but I don't follow the garment; I'm too entranced by the fire in Micah's eyes. By the way, he slaps his chest with an open palm over the place where his heart resides. "A man in love will move mountains to protect his family, and I paid off the right hospital personnel to move Joaquin to New York. No one knew outside of his wife and son, and Lionel only because he saw him before he fell unconscious. I wasn't going to let you try and get to him again. Neither of them."

"For her? I'm dying for her?" Incredulous. Snide.

"You'll die here being the miserable asshole you are because you broke my one rule, Diaz. She's untouchable." Shooting a hand out, Micah grabs him by the neck and brings him closer. Eye to eye. "You'll die because your son and his lover, Joseph, were going to sell you out. They had evidence in our deputy senator's laptop naming every illicit, filthy thing you've done. From embezzlement to beating your wife to the sexual assault of a female staff member at your office. That alone earns you a bullet to the head, but for thinking you can touch my wife, I want you to die slowly. Suffocating or eaten piece by piece by a bigger animal than you."

"How could…how did?"

"They hate you and my wife is an amazing woman with hacking skills no one can match." Rodolfo tries to look my way, but Micah tightens his hold. My husband's nails break his skin. "You don't look at her. You don't so much as breathe in her direction."

Diaz swallows hard, eyes wide. It's hitting home that there is truly no way out of this. "We can still work out a deal. You've had your revenge."

"Not even close." With that same hand and grip, he walks him to the very edge and throws him overboard. For thirty seconds, we wait in silence while faint sounds begin to be heard. Their calls take over, whistles and clicks of highly intelligent animals communicating while no human noises travel.

They're gone, and we have a future to begin.

A thought that hits Micah as well and his head snaps in my direction, chest breathing hard. The rest of the world will wait. What we've been through and explanations don't matter as I stand under the heated gaze of my soulmate in a pretty white dress, holding a rose.

"Do you, Liliana Rebel Armas, take me to be your husband." He stalks closer, each step sending a shiver of excitement through me. "For better or for poor. In sickness, death, and the occasional crime if the moment calls for it?"

"I do."

"Good. Because I do, too." His body is inches from mine and I'm yanked forward and into a solid, tanned chest. His other hand wanders from the curve of my ass and up my back to the dark strands of my hair flowing in the breeze. "I love it when you keep it long and wavy like this. You look like a goddess."

I'm blushing, but I can't help but ask, "So does that make you my god?"

"What I am is yours, Rebel. Today and always." Finding the split in my skirt, he pushes the fabric aside and bares me to the breeze.

I'm not wearing anything underneath, just like my top, the lace strategically fit to cover my nipples. "And this is mine."

His warm hand cups me, his palm rubbing against my clit, and I moan for him. Let him slide his fingers between my lips, spreading my wetness around before lifting me in his strong arms and carrying me toward the day bed set up beneath the darkening sky. It's decorated in soft, white linens and pillows, the comfortable mattress cushioning my body, but I can't focus on anything but the feel of him against me now.

The basket with oils and edible paints is forgotten.

The champagne with two long-stemmed flutes to toast to is cast aside.

Nothing outside of his naked body on mine makes sense, and I never want it to.

"Rip it off." My hand shakes, looking for the zipper of my top that starts near the underside of my left breast, but his hand stops me. The heat in his eyes holds me captive. "Please, Micah. I want to feel—"

"I want to remember you just like this, love." Slowly, he rubs the head of his cock through my folds. It's gentle. A little deeper each pass as his pre-come and my wetness mix, and the squelching sounds that follow are sinful. Obscene. More as he watches every single reaction, parting the light tulle and tucking it under my hip so it doesn't get in the way.

Then, there's the way he grits his teeth when I spread my legs wider to better cradle his hips. I'm his, and I want him to feel it in my every sigh. How I run my hands up his chest and then wrap my arms around his neck, pulling him down for a kiss.

It's slow at first. Pecks and nips, growing with intensity when he notches himself at my entrance and pushes just the tip inside. I can't control my clenching at the feel, how my body responds to his girth, and he growls into my mouth. Kissing me roughly. Possessively.

Our tongues meet and stroke, caressing each other while he pushes in another inch and this time, my nails dig into his shoulders.

I'm stretched to the point of pain, clinging to him, but I know he's not all the way in yet.

"I got you, baby." His voice is rough against my lips. His hands tremble as he grips my hip with one hand and the other slips beneath my neck, cupping it. "We'll take it slow."

I'm shaking my head before he's finished. "No. Just one thrust."

"Are you sure?"

"Yes."

"I love you, my Rebel. My life," he says, and I nod, but it's not enough for him. Micah stops moving and makes sure my eyes are on his. That every inch of his body is covering mine. "I take you, Liliana Armas, from this day forward as my wife. To have and to hold. For better or for worse." He kisses my lips, then cheeks, and finally my eyelids where a few tears have fallen. "For richer or for poorer. In sickness, health, hiding the fact a parent wasn't dead." That earns a laugh from me and he swallows hard. My walls haven't stopped trying to pull him in deeper. "I will honor, love, and cherish you for the rest of my life. Death will never part us."

"I love you, Micah Royce. Death will never part us."

"Then I now pronounce us husband and wife. I will now take what's mine."

"Please."

A single snap of his hips, and Micah's buried to the hilt. At first, it's a fiery shock to my senses—it hurts—but slowly it's replaced by a carnal need. Even though he's not moving and I'm acclimating to his girth, every few seconds his cock jerks inside of me, and I like the sensation.

How he feels. The little pleasurable ripples it sends throughout my body and I shift my hips beneath him, testing how it feels before doing it again. Each time teases a painful bliss, that same bite I enjoyed about anal and need more.

"I need you to move, Micah. Fuck me, baby."

"That mouth on you is one of my greatest weaknesses," he hisses, but gives me what I ask for, pulling out until just the tip sits at my entrance and thrusts back in. His eyes don't leave my face as he does this, watching for any discomfort, but he'll find none. Not the kind that says I want him to stop.

If anything, I want him to go harder, and as if reading my mind, the next snap of his hips causes me to gasp. It hits a delicious spot inside of me and I clench, eyes wide as he does it again. Then again. Micah sets the pace, and it's deep, long strokes—letting me feel every single ridge as he pulls out, and then I choke on a whimper when he slams in.

I'm clinging to him. Matching his pace, but then he bites my right nipple through the lace and my eyes roll back. The stinging sensation settles on my clit—I'm so wet for him I hear it with each thrust.

"Fuck, Rebel. My perfect girl." His lips trail up my neck and meet mine, the kiss now sloppy as each stroke brings me right to that precipice between pleasure and denial, one he's controlling. "Oh, fuck, yeah. Clench like that again."

"Please." My body thrums, every muscle tensing. "Please, Micah. I need—"

"Then come for your papi, good girl." Micah pushes my legs further apart, nearly touching the bedding before slipping his hands beneath my ass and with a cheek in each hand, he tilts my hips. "Let me feel you squeeze me before I fill you with my seed. Breed that pretty little cunt."

Between his words and the new angle, I come. It's long and building in intensity as he rides me through each pulse. I couldn't tell you where he ended or I began or when he found his own release, but I remember the feeling of him spilling inside of me.

The fullness. How right.

I also know that when the world came into focus and I could breathe again, he was still buried deep and had no plans of moving. Micah accommodated us in a way where I was wrapped up in his arms and warm. Sated and a little sleepy.

"Rest, baby. I'll be right here when you wake up, Mrs. Royce."

Epilogue 2
LILIANA

FAMILY MEETING...

"So, who wants to start?" Micah asks from beside me, hand on my thigh. We're at my father's home and sitting around the dining table a month after my wedding. It's a redo of the last one before the incident, to clear the air, and so far, no one's said a word. At least, not about what matters.

They look at me, and nothing. They look at each other, and nada.

And while it's been an amazing day and I'm proud of what I've accomplished since returning from our honeymoon, this is dampening my mood. Graduating with top honors, software and hardware patents for my firewall, and news I'll share in private with my husband later today—all of this should have me on cloud nine. I'm not. If anything, I'm annoyed.

They should not be messing with me right now.

"Well?" My eyes find Mom's and I raise a brow, just the way she taught me. That's always been her trait; the pursing of the lips follows closely at number two. "Why didn't you tell me in secret when you found out?"

She sighs, the exhale loud. "I know you're going to hate this, Mamita, but we simply couldn't."

"Again. Why?" I'm not going to back down, and as if sensing I'm pissed, Micah leans over and kisses my temple. "I deserve to know."

"She does," Lionel speaks up from beside Beatrice, who's been avoiding me. *Something happened there.* "It was hell for her."

"It was for all of us!" Mom thunders, tears gathering at the corner of her eyes. "Why do you want to keep reminding me of the worst pain—I can't."

"Then don't, and let someone else talk." It's spit out harshly, and she's taken aback. "Or did you think no one else felt his loss? The hole in my chest wouldn't let me breathe, and while I'm not angry at the fact it was hidden, I am by this attitude. At the least, I deserve to know my pain was worth it."

As soon as the words slip from me, I realize I've been holding back. That a part of me, minute as it is, feels betrayed. Not by Micah. We've talked—I know he did what was needed to save my father—but I just want everyone else to give me their side.

Am I being selfish?

"No, Lili. You're not...and yes, you said that out loud." Dad stands from his chair, shooting Mom a look. I've seen that one before. It's his *are you kidding me* expression. Even though he's still limping a bit and using a cane, Joaquin Armas tries to kneel by my chair.

"Are you crazy! Dad, no. Forget it...I'm—"

"Come here." Since I stopped Dad before he could kneel, Micah's given up his chair. He also helps his father-in-law sit. *My husband will be getting a little extra attention tonight.* "I can't wait to be done with all the physical therapy. Get more mobility back."

"It'll happen, my love. Trust the therapist." Mom's voice is full of emotion, but I avoid her and look down. Guess that's another thing I need to get used to. They've rekindled their relationship.

And while I'm excited about it—thrilled they're happy—can't she see I need this?

"I do, Celia, but I'll complain about that later." My hands are in my father's now and I'm given a soft yank into his side. The hug, though, is tight. "Look at me, Liliana." When I do, his smile is soft. His eyes hold nothing but love for me. "You are owed more than an explanation and I'm sorry everyone here has been avoiding it."

"Dad, I'm going to drop it. Don't—"

"Hush, kid." His reprimand makes me laugh, and out of the corner of my eye, I catch Mom standing from her seat. She moves to my other side, bending low enough to wrap an arm around my shoulders in an awkward hug since her husband is still holding me. We have to look funny, they're both almost cocooning me, but I need this. She still doesn't speak, though. "The accident was horrific, baby, and I'll never go into details with you about that, but please know it was *not* your fault."

Those words steal the air from my lungs, but before I can say anything, Micah shushes me. "Listen, baby. You need to hear this."

All I can do is nod; I'm unaware tears are falling down my cheeks until Dad's wiping under my eyes with a napkin. He's removed his arm but is turned to fully face me now. "Rodolfo, his son, and Joseph are at fault. They planned, lied, and tried to kill me. I'm here because Micah acted quickly—New York was a safe place for me to recover—even if that meant hiding the truth."

"But why?"

"You were being watched, Liliana," Mom says so low that I almost don't hear her. "Had you known and stopped grieving, they would've tried to take you—hurt you for information on his where-abouts—and I made the hard decision to keep it quiet."

"Micah would've protected me."

"Damn fucking right I would have, but she was in hysterics—"

"And you didn't want to fight and make it worse for her."

"Yes."

"Thank you." This brings me relief. I didn't know how much this simple explanation, to know it wasn't my fault, would bring me peace. "And I forgive you."

It'll take time to return to normalcy and for me to not doubt them, but it'll be okay. I have Micah in my corner now, and he's been warned.

This happens again, I'm on a *no pussy or ass or mouth* strike no matter what vows I took.

Epilogue 3
MICAH

∞♡

THREE MONTHS TO GO...

"**Y**ou will always be my biggest sin," I muse, running three fingers down my chin as I take in the sight on the screen. She's bent over and teasing me; her sinuous curves are on full display as I watch—access a hidden camera inside the frame of a painting right across from where she's currently touching her bare toes.

Every screen inside my home has remote access to her penthouse—a replica of mine, which I modeled with her in mind, because she has my complete attention every waking moment, even on days when physically, I'm away for work.

Seven days a week; this is how she accompanies me through my first cup of a sugary-sweet coffee. Naked and in bed through each sip, I follow the little sleep-rumbled rebel as she puts her hair up in one of those messy buns that makes me want to bite her. She's naturally beautiful. Moreover, it never fails to make my fingers twitch around the warm mug as the ever-present need to fuck her rides me:

This maddening desire to grip that bun and tug, undoing the mass of dark waves hidden, so I can position her mouth to my liking. Where I can nip and control—satiate the hunger that has clawed inside of me since the day I understood my protective instincts ran deeper than her being my best friend's little sister.

I've always wanted her, but I understood she was too young and needed time to grow and mature. To make her dreams come true. To run so I could chase her around like the addicted beast I am.

But now, she's all woman. Smart and warm with a sassy mouth meant to rob me of function, which Liliana does without fail every single day. My cock throbs only for her. A desire I never let anyone satisfy because doing so would be blasphemy—to curse what we are.

"It's my honor to love this woman." Vow made. Vow kept.

And I've rewarded my good behavior by stalking her every move.

"… so tight this morning," she grits out, and my attention snaps back to her session. Liliana standing upright now, twisting right to left—four times she does this—before extending both hands up toward her ceiling.

Now, I'm gifted a front view while she's arching, thrusting her chest forward in a lavender-colored sports bra that does little to hide her beaded nipples. They're tight and their outline through the thin fabric makes my mouth water—cock dribbling a little pre-come across my bare abdomen while it jerks in need of her touch.

Yet I don't touch myself. Not when she reaches for her phone and taps on the screen, changing her playlist to something with a more upbeat sound. The thrum of an island beat fills her home and mine, and a smile tugs at my lips.

While doing yoga, most choose something calming or classical, but not my rebel. My girl sways her hips and dips low once, making her asscheeks clap a few times before placing her cell down and then reaching for a small tension band nearby. Slipping into it, she keeps it mid-thigh before turning and once again gifting me the perfect view of her backside.

Slim back and two dimples right above the swell of her ass; she's tight and curvaceous while her stature makes her pocket-sized for my own convenience. It's a turn-on how small she is compared to my over six-foot-four frame. How easily she fits right under my arms, the crown of her head barely reaching my upper chest.

"Bend for me, baby. Show me what's mine." As if she's heard me, Liliana does just that. She grips the back of her calves and bends forward, folding herself in half until her large breasts touch her thighs but careful not to add too much pressure, and then holds the position. The lavender material of her yoga pants, the same as her bra, stretches across her ass to the point it's almost see-through and I can just make out the lips of her cunt.

No panties. Nothing but that fabric and her stretching while completely unaware I'm watching. *Son of a bitch.* One day I'm going to take her just like this. Cut those pants and make her sing for me.

I want her whimpers and her tears.

I want her screams and the scores of her nails down my back.

Another harsh jerk of my dick and my balls grow heavy; I count with her. For sixty seconds, I watch her take in deep breaths and let them out slowly before parting her legs a little and adjusting the band so it's higher up her thighs. Once satisfied, she places the tips of her fingers on the floor while careful to keep her balance.

This is how her routine always begins; my girl is a creature of habit and quickly moves into a chair position, lowering herself in increments until she's almost in a full yogi squat. This is done three times before slipping into a downward and then upward dog, keeping her abdomen a little off the ground and breathing evenly through each set until ending this phase with a plank pose. Each one is held longer than the last until perspiration starts to slowly form on her temples. A few beads roll down, while wayward strands slip from her top knot and stick to the now-slick skin at the base of her flushed neck.

As the last pose, she chooses a corpse position, and this is where she begins her daily prayer.

"Padre nuestro que estas en el Cielo, santificado sea tu nombre..." Liliana's sweet voice comes through the speaker of my TV, and I follow along with her in the Lord's prayer. I match her Spanish with the English version until we say *Amen* together.

And no sooner than we do, my alarm goes off and my phone buzzes with an incoming text, causing the device to vibrate. It shakes atop the sheets, and it's her mother's name across the screen.

> Don't you dare be late, Micah. Three o'clock on the dot. ~Celia

"Was that Mom? Cause she just messaged me too." Her voice causes my head to snap up, my reason for living standing a few feet from me. "That connection really comes in handy, Papi. Did you like the show?"

"Come here." A demand. A groan.

Because there's something so incredibly sexy about my pregnant wife—all sweaty and flushed—teasing me by letting me watch her workouts. This entire floor, her unit and mine, have become our playground since I showed her where every single camera is. Since she realized the lengths I've gone to always keep my eyes on her.

And fuck me if the little brat wasn't turned on by it. Sucked my cock like the perfect little slut she is for me.

Horny. Needy. Whimpering.

"No."

"I can't hear you from across the room, Liliana. Come a little closer."

"Now why would I do that?" The sports bra has a zipper in the front and she's quick to pull it down, revealing her tits to me slowly. "You like to watch, not play. Maybe I'll go back next door and lock...shit!"

Rebel takes off laughing as I chase her, running back the way she came and heading toward the other penthouse. Not that she makes it far; I have Liliana in my arms before the sneaky thing can make it past our wedding pictures—the ones we can't show our families.

These were all her choices, too.

Her blood on my cock after our first time.

Her ass stretched around my dick while the moon was high.

The morning after, her in my arms smiling at the camera while I slept beside her.

And it's right in front of those three that I bend her over, hands on the wall below the frame with my cock, and I rip a hole in her yoga pants. She opens her mouth to yell, more than likely to complain they're expensive, but it turns into whimpers as I run the fat head through her slick slit twice.

She's dripping for me, thighs wet and core clenching, and I slam in to the hilt without warning. I'm careful she doesn't lose her balance, both hands on her hips as I ride her hard, not stopping while those pretty little cries I adore reverberate throughout the space.

"Oh shit, Micah!" Motherfuck, my name on her lips is heaven. More so when Rebel's clenching hard, her cunt trying to pull me in deeper. Hold me inside of her. "Baby, I'm so close."

"Then come for me. Mark your Papi, Rebel." Slipping a hand around her front, I cup one of her breasts before pinching her nipple. These days they're sensitive and make her pussy tighter around my girth, but today, it's a little more. The harder I pull, the more she tenses and I slap the tip hard, knowing she needs the sting. "That's it, wife. Come all over my cock."

Her orgasm forces mine, milking me as her walls tighten and throb, pulling each drop. I fill her to the brim, loving how she cries out for more. How she wants me to cuddle her right after, head lolled back and complaining as I pull out.

And while I'd love nothing more than to stay buried to the hilt while she naps, we have a baby shower to get to in our new home.

We were kicked out by our mothers and decided to come here and relax for a bit.

"Come on, love. They're waiting on us."

"But a nap!" Her whine causes me to chuckle, and she tilts her face my way; I get the stink eye. "I'm tired, Micah. No one likes a grumpy pregnant woman."

"Now it's Micah? What happened to Papi?"

"Let your wife sleep. Happy life."

"They have a tower of guava and cheese turnovers just for you, baby. Do you want them to get stale?" That perks her up and I'm being shoved aside, left to watch her waddle away and back to my old penthouse with my come dripping down her thighs. As always, my heart thumps harshly inside my chest at the sight of her and my cock stiffens to full mast again.

My hunger for her will never be sated, but what I can do is live to protect what's mine.

My love for her will never wane. It only grows, and I'll forever worship her for giving me her heart. For carrying my son.

"Baby, I don't hear the water running."

A huff from just beyond the closet makes my lips twitch. "Bite me!"

Striding toward my bedroom, I give my cock a tight squeeze as I catch her on our bed, snuggled under the covers. I accept we're going to be late and there will be complaints. I come to terms with the fact that I'll always drop everything to keep the devious grin she's currently giving me on her face. *Guess she needs that nap after all.*

"You know damn fucking well I bite, Rebel."

The End For Now...

Lionel and Beatrice's story coming 2024

Want more of Thiago De Leon and his sexy, dirty mouth? Read his story in Mine, Beautiful Sinners Series (Book 3)

Blurb:

In Miami, I'm royalty. The beginning and the end.
I'm the truth my queen will never escape.

Thiago Rivera De Leon doesn't believe in second chances, and I never show mercy to those stupid enough to cross me. Loyalty wins you favors but trying to overthrow the city's king will find you with one of my bullets between the eyes.

A simple promise I always keep while abiding by two rules:

I don't forgive. I don't forget.

And after spending the last five years behind bars, I'm out with two goals in mind...

Kill the bastards responsible.

Reclaim my Luna.

Buy Link:
https://books2read.com/u/3Ray8G

Coming Nov. 2023

Pre-Order: https://books2read.com/omission-fates-bite
Goodreads: https://www.goodreads.com/book/show/123282316-omission

One look into her warm violet eyes and my world stops.
She's where I begin and now end. The prize at the end of my battles
—who I will k*ll for.

"Mate."

ABOUT THE AUTHOR

Elena M. Reyes was born and raised in Miami, Florida. She is the epitome of a Floridian and if she could live in her beloved flip-flops, she would.

As a small child, she was always intrigued with all forms of art— whether it was dancing to island rhythms, or painting with any medium she could get her hands on. Her first taste of writing came to her during her fifth-grade year when her class was prompted to participate in the D. A. R. E. Program and write an essay on what they'd learned.

Her passion for reading over the years has amassed her with hours of pleasure. It wasn't until she stumbled upon fanfiction that her thirst to write overtook her world. She now resides in Central Florida with her husband and son, spending all her down time letting her creativity flow and characters grow.

Website: https://www.elenamreyes.com/

Find My Books Here:
https://www.bookbub.com/authors/elena-m-reyes

Email: Reyes139ff@gmail.com

facebook.com/ElenaMReyesAuthor

x.com/ElenaMReyes

instagram.com/elenar139

tiktok.com/@authorelenamreyes

bookbub.com/profile/elena-m-reyes

ALSO BY ELENA M. REYES

ALSO, BY ELENA M. REYES

SERIES:

FATE'S BITE SERIES

LITTLE LIES

LITTLE MATE

HALF TRUTHS DUET

HALF TRUTHS: THEN

HALF TRUTHS: NOW

OMISSION (NOV 2023)

SERIES:

BEAUTIFUL SINNER SERIES

Each book is a standalone.

Now Live!

SIN (#1)

COVET (#2)

MINE (#3)

YOURS (#4)

RISQUE #5

OWN #6

Beautiful Sinner Spin-Off

CORRUPT

MY SINFUL VALENTINE

(Marked Series)

Marking Her #1

Marking Him #2

Scars #2.5

Marked #3

(I Saw You)

I Saw You

I Love You #1.5

Teasing Hands Duet

Teasing Hands #1

Taunting Lips #2

SAFE ROMANCE:

Taste Of You

Doctor's Orders

Back To You

STANDALONES:

Craving Sugar

Stolen Kisses